Eye Spy

Harper's Beginning

Book 1

Written By:
Lailah Clayborne and Kallie Harris

Illustrated By:
Kallie Harris

Revision Publishing LLC
www.revisionpub.com

Published by Revision Publishing LLC

EDUCATION·COURSES·RESOURCES

To little writers everywhere

—Lailah and Kallie

Prank Backfire

"Ms. Ellison can you explain what happened?" Principal Kaleb demanded more than asked. I don't like him that much; he's always throwing me eagle eyes, and he leaves campus all the time, but it seems as if he is always there when I mess up.

"Ms. Ellison!" he repeated.

"Nothing, Mr. Kaleb." That wasn't exactly the truth, but I couldn't afford to have my grandmother come and pick me up again.

"I am getting impatient, Ms. Ellison." He started to tap his shoe on the floor.

"Uh...I just—it was an accident."

He pinched the bridge of his nose and sighed. "Harper Ellison, it is always an accident with you."

I rolled my eyes. "I'm telling the truth! Seriously! She tripped. I'm serious. I just so happened to be standing where she was," I complained.

"All right. That's it. I will be calling your grandmother. You can wait in the front office." He motioned toward the green door that said, "YOU KNOW BETTER NOW." (It should say, "NOW YOU CAN LEAVE IN SHAME AND DO IT ALL AGAIN.") I walked as slowly as possible through his boring office. Brown walls, brown shelves on the walls, brown pencils, brown desk... brown everything. The only spot of color was his door and a potted plant in the far corner; it's almost invisible. Such a boring person.

It had been almost half an hour before Grams honked her horn.

In fifteen seconds, she honked the horn
again. I had to scramble to get all of my
things in time before she started screaming
through the window. I pulled open the door
and sat in the front seat. The car didn't
move until I started talking. "Grams, I...I'm

sorry. It—I..." She just looked at the road and hummed a song.

"You can take this up with your parents, Harper," she finally said once we pulled into the driveway. Our house is really nice—two stories, it's brown on the outside but pretty fun on the inside, blue walls...lots of stuff better than Mr. Kaleb's. The house was silent and empty. No one was here except for Umma, who jumped up and down at my feet.

"Hi there, Umma. Be careful of my new shirt, you can't slobber on it." Umma, my dog, is like a support animal for me. She trotted out to the backyard and went chasing the squirrel that comes for snacks from my little brother.

"Go do your homework."

Grams went to the *casita* in the back. She has lived there ever since Gramps died—she never talks about him, though. When I ask her if she wants to talk about it, she shoos me away and says she's fine. I finished my work—kinda—and slipped into my room. Now that I really looked at it, I realized my room was in need of a makeover. My green walls needed a new coat, my floor needed to be cleaned, and I needed new blankets and sheets. Seeing my room this way made me feel weird.

"Harper, I'm home!" Mom yelled from the front door.

"Mom—" She shot me a look. "*Mami*, why are you home so early?" My mom works as a vet and is usually home later in the evening for some reason. She is Mexican, and my dad is African American. Since I speak English at school, my mom thinks that I am forgetting my Mexican heritage, so she wants me to speak more Spanish at home.

"*¡Tengo buenas noticias!*" ("I have good news!") she said. My mom speaks fluent Spanish, and I don't. I can barely say a full sentence, but I understand it.

"What's the good news?"

5

She smiled excitedly and put her groceries down on the counter. An earpiece fell out of her ear. "What's that?" I asked.

"Oh, this? I was on a call in the car. *Anyway,* I will share at dinner, when your father is here." She shoved the milk into our fridge. "Where is *Abuela*?" Mom asked.

"In her casita," I said. "What's for dinner?" She doesn't like when I ask her questions like that, but I don't like to eat the school lunch, so I'm hungry most of the time when I get home.

"You'll see, hija." She shooed me away.

"Mami, I'm bored," I complained.

She knitted her eyebrows. "Look around, go outside, clean—we could use some cleaning around here." She nodded to herself.

I hesitated. "Speaking of cleaning...I want to redo my room, Mami." She shrugged. "What does that mean?" I asked.

"You want to redo your room, eh? Get yourself a job. You think I pay the bills by begging my mami to work extra?" She shook her head and started washing dishes.

"You sound like Abuela," I grumbled and grabbed my dad's old computer and walked out onto the front porch and sat down.

I tried searching for jobs online, but none of the options made sense to me. Within ten minutes, I gave up. I sat out on the porch for a while until a dirty orange school bus screeched down our driveway and Simon came running out of the bus door.

"Harper! I got an award for best behavior! Unlike, well, *you*," he bragged. He's such a Goody Two-shoes. He gets good reports from the principal—which, like he said, is unlike me. He ran into the house and I could hear mom congratulating him and promising him extra churro cheesecake tonight. I sprinted down the side of the house to Grams's casita. Her door was closed and locked, so I had to peek through the window. She was reading the book my dad gave her for Mother's Day last year and munching on a mango. She looked up and almost spotted me. I ducked and rolled to the side.

"Come in my little nieta!" Grams said. Grams is Mom's mom, so she is also a fluent

Spanish speaker.

I remembered my training and shakily spoke, *"Vale, vale."* Then I gave up. "You caught me."

She opened the door and set down her mango. "What do you need, *nieta*?" she asked. She is really fun, but when she feels something, she feels it strongly. I didn't want her to get mad at me for complaining, so I started off with the thing I knew she wouldn't get annoyed with me for.

"I am bored. Mo—Mami—says that I should clean, but I don't feel like it, and Simon is bragging about how he is getting good reports at school," I said without complaint, as more of a statement.

"You are older than him, right?" she asked expectantly.

"Si," I said.

"So why do you care if he brags?" I didn't have the answer to that. So she continued. "And why don't you go and pull a prank on your brother? That's entertaining. Or go help your mami cook," she said.

I am *no* good in the kitchen, and I *didn't* have the energy to waste good material on something this small. I nodded like I was going to do one of these activities and walked out. I sat in my room and took my secret stuffed rhino out of my closet (which I keep cluttered to hide him).

"Raymond Rhino, I missed you. But I'm *bored*," I whispered. To my surprise, Umma was watching me. I hadn't even noticed her when I walked in my room. I shoved my rhino under the clutter and rolled my eyes. "Umma, please don't tell anyone. You know there was a connection between us when I was younger, and I am too old to have a rhino. Yet here we are." Umma put her paw on my journal. I should have known; she has always been the deal type. She never just focused on one thing, she always had one eye on something else. When I say always, I mean ALWAYS.

I didn't have a secret that she didn't know. How she did it, I didn't know.

"Fine."

I, Harper Ellison, am swearing to Umma that I will give her an extra treat every day after school if she keeps my secret.

Harper Ellison

I had no choice but to do this because Umma was a BEAST when she wasn't rewarded for what she does. She ratted me out a few months earlier when I broke my brother's spelling bee trophy and hid it in my drawer. She was there when it happened, and I told her not to tell. But I didn't give her anything in return, so when my family figured out that the trophy was missing, she led them to where I hid it. After that, Mom had me on gardening duty for two months. And I'm sure that Simon was enjoying sipping on apple juice and watching me pick weeds.

I handed the paper to Umma, and she took it to her dog bed, where she hides things. Then I heard loud footsteps entering the house—I recognized the sound of boots.

It was Dad. "Hello, family!" he called.

"*Hola, mi amor.*" Mom swung in front of him, and they immediately started dancing through the kitchen. I love watching my parents dance; they always tell us stories of when they were dating. Sometimes it's *disgusting!* They started talking about one summer night when they were dancing.

"We were both so nervous! You were next up on stage," my dad started.

"I remember that," Mom said. Within three minutes they were giggling and laughing. So I cleared my throat.

"Ahem, excuse me, love birds," I said. My mom froze and scolded me about how I shouldn't interrupt adult conversations.

"Okay, jeez!" I skipped over to my dad. "Hi, Dad! How was work?" I asked.

He sighed and brushed his oil-stained jacket. "Well, work was okay. Nothing new." My dad works as an engineer for skyscrapers. He always comes home late, and mom gives him foot massages to calm him.

"Oh! My enchiladas!" Mom went to check the oven, which immediately burst out a black cloud of smoke.

Grams came in and kissed dad on the cheek. *"Ya esta lista la cena?"* ("Is dinner ready yet?") Grams asked.

"Almost," my mom said.

"Go wash up." My dad gestured towards me and my brother.

Simon yelled out, "I bet I can beat you up the stairs!" I rolled my eyes and went up the staircase.

"Hurry up," Grams said, "I'm sure you could beat him up there!" But Simon was already coming down.

I raised an eyebrow at Grams as she shrugged at me.

"You should have been faster!" She threw her hands up and walked away.

I washed my hands quickly and went down the stairs. My mom was putting a plate on the table that had her cheesecake on it. I reached for my chair and pulled it out, reluctantly. I really, *really* needed to change seats. My usual seat is right next to Simon. He is the messiest eater in the world. I tried my best to scoot closer and closer to Grams, who sat beside me.

"*Muevete* Harper, give me some space to eat," she said, pushing me away. I had no choice. I was stuck with Simon. Mom placed the enchilada platter in the center, and I went grabbing for the biggest one that wasn't halfway burnt. I could see the beans and cheese squeezing out.

But then Simon reached and took it right when I was a millimeter away.

"Hey! You saw me taking that one!" I yelled.

"Nuh-uh!" He licked it all around.

"*Eww!* You nasty pig! Aren't you getting extra churro cheesecake?" I scolded. He filled himself up with crocodile tears.

"Harper, I know you wanted that one, but Simon got it. Here." Dad passed me the biggest taquito on the table. I took it—reluctantly—and bit into it. I didn't want to show it, but I was satisfied.

Right when I was about to thank my dad, a big squirt of beans, cheese, chicken, and tomato sauce hit me in the face.

"Simon! *¿Por qué le hiciste eso a tu hermana?*" ("Why would you do that to your sister?") Mom said.

"*Discúlpate de inmediato.*" ("Apologize at once.") Grams pointed her finger at him.

"Sorry, Harper. It was an accident, I won't do it again." He kicked me under the table.

"Anyhow, I have some good news to share," Mom said. "I got a promotion at work!" My mom works as a vet and always tells us about her patients. "I am now the lead surgeon!" She smiled, and Dad gave her a kiss.

"Fantastic!" Grams hugged Mom.

I told Mom that it was awesome that she got promoted, but Simon ruined the moment when he "accidentally" spilled his milk all over my brand-new shirt. I got up fast and ran to the bathroom to get it off before it stained. I heard Mom, Dad, and Grams talking to Simon. "Shame on you!" Mom's voice said. I opened the door a crack just to see what was happening. Simon was refilling his milk!

He ruined my outfit, stole my enchilada, *and* he didn't even wipe my seat! I went upstairs to change my shirt, then went back downstairs, bringing down my shirt to remind everyone of what Simon did. I needed revenge. I finally found a good reason to use my materials! I finished my food really fast so I could prepare. I made slime, I went outside and collected a bucketful of sand from our sandy backyard, and I found my old rubber spider. This was going to be *good*.

At about 11:00 pm I got out of bed and snuck into Simon's room. Mom was in her bed asleep, and Dad was, too. Grams was in her casita doing who knows what, and Simon was fast asleep. I crawled down on the floor, opened up my slime and poured it into his morning slippers. Then I took the rubber spider and hung it right over him so that when he woke up, he'd be scared. Finally, I took the sand and put it inside of his school shoes. My work was done. I smirked and crawled my way out of his room.

The next morning, I got up and shook off my sleepy energy. I went through my drawers, and it came down to two outfits. This was where Raymond the Rhino came out. I locked my door and scanned the room for Umma. *Nope*, I thought. I grabbed him and sat him on my bed.

"Okay, Raymond, which one?" I held up overalls with a pink watermelon crop and a flannel dress with blue leggings. He took his precious time and finally chose the flannel with leggings. "You're right, Raymond, I'll look super childish if I come to school wearing overalls and pink, especially on a

Friday. You are so smart," I said. Once I got dressed, I peeked in Simon's room.

He was still asleep. I got up before everyone because I deserved to see this. By the time I was done, I still had five minutes until my family woke. I sat by my brother's room and waited. I was so anxious to see his face; it was the longest five minutes of my life.

Finally, the time was here and all I heard was, *"AHHHHHHHHHHHH!"* Things went downhill from there. Mom and Dad came running down the hallway and raced past me into Simon's room. He must've screamed too loud because Grams came in with her rollers, neighbors knocked at the door, and Umma came darting out of Mom and Dad's room as fast as lightning. Grams speed walked into Simon's room, saw the rubber spider hanging from the ceiling and got so scared she backed up and stepped on Umma's tail. Umma started to howl-bark-cry so loud, Simon started crying louder, Grams's voice was in the mix of it all saying sorry to Umma, Mom was practically yelling at Simon asking him what had happened. The noise from outside went from knocking to police sirens. Am I gonna get arrested? I seemed to shrink into the wall. Then a pounding at the door made everything stop. Mom strode out of the room and dad took her place silently asking Simon what happened. Mom opened the door to police officers armed with guns and everything. "We were called due to a possibly endangered child and or break in," one officer said while the other circled our house with off limits tape. I peeked into Simon's room and saw tears coming down his cheeks, slime covering his feet, and the spider on his forehead. For a moment I felt sorry for him.

"I'm so sorry, this was just an accident," my mom explained to the police officers. "Just a bad dream or something like that." She glared at me and continued talking. She knew I did this.

"Aw, man, I'm in so much trouble!" I whispered.

The police had to check the house and make sure that nothing *else* had happened. I had to admit what I did, and Simon had to explain what happened to him, but I wasn't able to hear because they took him to his room. I sat in the kitchen once things settled down, and Mom sat a huge plate of *huevos rancheros* near Simon and gave me a few pieces of mango and one of the most burnt enchiladas from last night.

"That's what you get for causing such an *escandalo broma*!" ("scandalous prank") Mom told me. It went on like that for the rest of the week. Finally, on Saturday, I grabbed my phone and started to text Chrissy. She's my best friend and she has been since, well... third grade! I texted her:

I played a prank on that pesky little Simon and the whole neighborhood came and the police did 2.

She texted me back three minutes later, saying she'd heard about that:

Yeah, a few minutes ago the police reported that a sister pranked her brother AND stole a piggy bank!

I pinched myself. HARD. I couldn't believe they were accusing me of theft! I had to get out of there! "Mami, can we take a vacation to Mexico?" I asked.

"*¡Niña! ¡No se lo que estas pensando!*" ("Child! I don't know what you are thinking!") Mom said, scrunching up her eyebrows. "You are *supposed* to be on punishment, plus, People don't just run off on a vacation like some kind of wild animals migrating. These things need to be planned, I'm sorry Harper. But no."

"I—I want to learn more about my Mexican ancestors." At that, Mom's expression changed completely, and she went and grabbed a suitcase from the closet.

"Oh I'm so glad that you finally want to learn about your past to affect your future! I love you, I love you! Kisses, kisses!" Mom actually bought it. "*¡Nos vamos a México! ¡Vamos, mi familia! We are going to Mexico!* Come on, my family! We must pack! Pack!!"

We hadn't booked flights, we hadn't made any real plans yet, but when it came to appreciating our Mexican heritage, Mom had a one-track mind. I did as she said, and started to pack.

"Bathing suit...oh, this shirt looks amazing...ripped jeans...I think this is in style...oh, yeah, I need this dress," I said to myself.

My phone went off, and it was Chrissy calling me. "Hello? Yeah, hi Chris. We're going to Mexico. No, I'm not joking! I'm going. Bye." I hung up. Sure, it seemed crazy to leave for Mexico with zero planning or notice, but given how bad things had gotten for me after my prank, it seemed even crazier to stay right now. I needed to find somewhere to hide away while all this calmed down, and Mexico was the perfect place. I looked around, wrapped Raymond in my flannel dress, then stuffed him—and my dress—in my suitcase. Finally, I packed my plane pack—the bag I put my snacks and stuff in. I put in my iPhone and headphones.

"Here I come, Mexico!"

Mexico

The next week, when I came downstairs, my mom was on the phone with the school: "Yes. I am calling for Harper Ellison…"

She raised her eyebrows, "Of course. Give me a second." She held the phone to her chest. "Why didn't you tell me you caused an incident at school? You are lucky we have already planned."

I whispered, "A lot happened last week." She shrugged and picked the phone back up. "OK, I'm here. Hello, Mr. Kaleb. I am aware. We've discussed it. Yes. So I was just calling to say that Harper will be absent for the week. She is visiting family in Mexico. Okay then. I'll see you next, week." She hung up the phone. "I will let the 'incident' slide just because you want to go learn more about your Mexican heritage." I kinda felt bad about lying to my mom, but at least I would be able to get a break from all of this drama.

"Yeah, where are we staying?" I asked.

"With your Tío Mateo." She dialed another number into her phone. "Hello, Dr. V, I spoke with Ryan last week about...Oh! He told you, great. I just wanted you to get the message. Good, but could you keep my dog, Umma?" My mom continued. Dr. V is her boss, and she is super nice. Simon came down into the living room and saw that I was there; he stopped and glared at me until I left the room. Talk about someone who holds grudges.

I went to Grams's casita and knocked on the door. "*Ven*," she said.

"Are you excited to see Tío Mateo in Mexico?" I asked.

She folded a shirt with a picture of a flower on it and smiled. "Nieta, I am very, very, *emocionada* to see my young Mateo." She never seemed this happy before. That guilt that was inside of me melted away as I watched Grams talk on and on about how excited she was to see Uncle Mateo. "It has been a while since I've seen my little child, you know; it was three years ago, the last time I saw my Mateo, yes that's right. I moved here three years ago. Mateo stayed to take care of his wife." She grinned and grabbed for a necklace.

"Tío Mateo is married?" I asked. I never thought of him as the marriable type. Last time I saw him, was when I was nine, he had peach fuzz and silky, straight black hair that he always wore parted to one side with the other part shaved. He had those collared shirts that he called his *"originales lujosas"* ("fancy originals"), and he let me try on one that had a butterfly on the pocket. He called that one his *"receptor de trabajo"* ("job catcher").

"Used to be married," she said flatly.

"What do you mean, *'used to be married'*?" I asked.

"That is not a child's business, nieta," she said firmly. "Now let's not think about that." She brightened.

"Emilia, Harper, come on, we are leaving," Dad called from the back door.

"Okay, okay, Ron," Grams called back. I ran past her and grabbed all of my bags.

"So we booked a flight and everything, right? 'Cause I learned in school that people that don't book flights aren't able to get on the plane, Dad." Simon said. I rolled my eyes.

"Yes, Simon, of course we booked a flight," Mom said.

"Duh, you think we are *that* unprepared?" I added. Dad glared at me through the rear mirror as we drove to the airport. "I mean, *of course, little Simon.* They are so *doubtful* at this age," I said to please Mom and Dad. Then I pulled him in by his ear and whispered, "I know why Dum-Dums are your favorite candy now."

We stopped by Mom's office and dropped off Umma. It took forever since Mom was talking to her boss before even mentioning Umma. We got in the car (finally) and I got on my phone and started playing Imposter, a video game, for a little bit. I saw another player there called Simon. There are millions of people who play that game, so I didn't think too much of it. When I became a ghost, Simon stuck his tongue out at me. The little squirt was actually playing! I'd give him a piece of my mind if I didn't have this seat belt on!

I think Grams saw how Simon and I were looking at each other because she interfered. "Simon, *ven aqui y mira esta vista afuera*" ("come here and look at this view outside"). Even though it was just the blindingly bright sun sitting there, Simon turned to his window and stared at the trees passing by.

"We're here." Dad sounded relieved. "Traffic is busy on a Friday evening," he said.

"This doesn't look like the airport, Dad." I said as we pulled into the driveway.

"We are at your cousin's house. They will take care of our car while we are gone, and the Zuber will be here any minute," Mom explained. Cousin Gabriella walked out onto the front porch and waved to us. She's like nineteen years old, but she stays home all the time. I can tell why my parents thought this would be a good idea.

"*Hola familia, ¿cómo estás?*" ("Hello family, how are you?") she asked.

"*¿Bien, y tu?*" ("Good, and you?") Mom said as she stepped in for a hug.

"*Estoy bien, ahora tengan un buen viaje*" ("I'm fine, now you have a good trip").

Our Zuber pulled into the driveway. The Zuber car was rusty and old, the outside was peeling, and it smelled like gas. The driver was a hippie, wore a tie-dye tux and had long, black, frizzy hair. "Wassup, dudes?" he said with a little drowsy sound in his voice.

"Uh...hello." Mom checked her phone and whispered to Dad, "THIS is the Zuber driver? This is not who I thought I saw in the profile picture." She forced a smile and opened the door. The inside was a little better than the outside—the seats were pale and had little blotches of tie dye in spots.

"There isn't enough room for all of us," Grams said.

"I know. Ron, go get in the front. Simon, sit on Harper's lap, and I'll sit in the middle. Your mother will sit by me," Grams ordered. I immediately threw my hands up. I didn't want this weasel on my lap! Grams held up one finger shushing me.

"It's all good, dudes! The little bro can sit on my lap!" the Zuber driver said excitedly, yet somehow *still* sounding drowsy.

Mom scrunched up her nose and made a disgusted look, then spoke in Spanish so our Zuber driver wouldn't understand. "¡Este extraño no se acercará a mi dulce bebé!" ("This stranger will not come close to my sweet baby boy!")

"Fine," I said, rolling my eyes. "I'll make room for Simon, but I WON'T let him *on* my lap."

I threw Simon into the trunk. He pulled me in, and my seat was immediately filled by Dad, who dreamily stared at Mom—or maybe he was relieved to not have to sit in the front, but I think that he was trying to get his attention off of this stinky dump of a car.

"All right. I guess that we're stuck here," I said, looking at Simon. "We need to get out of here fast," Grams said to the Zuber driver.

"No problemo, bros and broettes." He started to go sixty miles per hour. Once on the freeway he started speeding over a hundred miles an hour.

Simon was tumbling around in the trunk. He jumped over the chairs and said, "Are you a race car driver?"

"Totally, little bro!" the Zuber driver said. We were at the airport in a snap. When I looked over the seats, I saw Mom holding her chest with her eyes wide open, and Grams was holding onto Mom and Dad.

We got on our plane. I sat next to Grams, but that was a bad idea because she fell asleep as soon as we started flying. Grams snores, so I couldn't hear my movie that well. I watched some weird movie about a spy agency. (Talk about corny!)

I heard the pilot say over the speaker, "Alrighty, folks, we have turbulence coming up, so fasten those seatbelts! Our team is coming with pretzels. Enjoy the ride! Oh, and don't use the earbuds. We can't afford another ear infection based law suit." I grinned at the thought of me having my own.

I fell asleep two hours in. The flight was

silent until we hit turbulence. Grams and I woke up and saw that we were still in the air. I saw Mom and Dad asleep and Simon was putting pretzel crumbs in someone's hair. The flight attendant saw the pretzel incident and took Simon out of the section we were in.

She asked the pilot something, then we heard over the voiceover, "OK everyone, we have a child who was playing a small prank. Come and get 'em if he's yours. He has curly black-brown hair and brownish tan skin... oh, and he says he's lost two teeth." Mom immediately stood up from her sleep and said some things under her breath-that I'd rather not mention-as she stomped down the aisle.

"Oh, boy." Grams said when she saw my mom.

"What's wrong, Grams?" I asked. She shook her head. "Your mother, nieta. When she gets like that..." She exhaled. I knew what she meant right away. One time my dad forgot their anniversary, and my mom was so mad I think she locked *herself* in her room to protect us all from herself. She didn't talk to us for the rest of the night, and she stress-ate late at night. That was a bad day for Dad. His nightly foot massages were done by me, and to be honest, my mom has to really love him to deal with that. My mom tried to act all civilized when she grabbed Simon by the arm and took him to the restroom. She came out, and Simon came out. For the rest of the flight, he was sitting still in his seat and didn't even look out the window, he just stared at the seat in front of him. *Creepy.*

"What do you think Mami did to him?" I asked Grams. She shrugged.

"I don't know. She probably talked the daylights out of that brother of yours- or worse." She started back getting ready to get into her sleeping position. I wanted to see if mom *looked* okay. I threw my pretzel bag on the floor towards Mom so I could sneak a look at her.

"Oh, I seemed to have dropped my bag on the floor! Lemme pick it up now!" I said comically. Then, I saw Mom's face. It is not *humanly possible* to describe. She was REALLY mad and she was smiling *extremely* wide.

I also noticed that Dad was fanning her. It was... INTERESTING. I quickly picked up my pretzel bag and went back to sleep, or at least I tried to. The little white roses on the neck pillow that came with the seat were so itchy, I woke up in ten minutes and there were still three hours left on the flight. I watched a movie.

Soon, the pilot started to talk again. "OK, hope you all had a good time. We are experiencing landing turbulence, fasten up and sit back, we'll be down in a few minutes." Being on the ground again sounded amazing. The airplane wasn't all that great, and Raymond was still in the bottom of the plane.

The landing turbulence was really strong; I felt like I was going to fall out of my seat. Simon hadn't moved the rest of the flight, and as far as I could see, he hadn't gone to the restroom either. I think he was scared of it. "Passengers, we have hit the ground, please do not exit until we have hit a complete stop." The pilot said. When we finally did pull to a stop, people seemed to be fighting to get out of there. When I tried to unbuckle, my dad signaled me to stay where I was.

"Stay right there, Harper. We can't afford a missing child," he said to me. I could tell he wanted to add, "And we also can't afford another mom monster," but he wouldn't say it in front of her. Once everyone was out of the plane, we finally left.

"*Vamos, mi hija*," Mom said to me in a strained voice. Her cheeks were red from smiling so hard.

"Are you okay, Mami?" I asked when we exited baggage claim and headed out to the front.

"*Sí*. Of course! Why wouldn't I be? I mean everyone is fine, I'm FINE! Stop getting in grown people's business!" She spoke fast and firmly.

"Uh...okay?" I knew she would need some persuading to get back into shape. "I just can't wait to remember my Mexican ancestors!" I said a little too loudly. She perked up and put on a real smile.

"Yeah, Harper, you should be." Dad looked like a weight was lifted off of his shoulders when Mom really smiled. I looked over at Simon; he walked in a straight line and looked right ahead of himself. Mom seemed to notice.

"Oh, come here, my son," she said, sounding sorry. He inched closer and closer then finally hugged her. Dad and Simon looked the same—like a weight had been lifted off of their shoulders. I approached the door to where another Zuber would pick us up. The view of Mexico was really nice from the airport, palm trees and fruit trees. When I opened the door, a sweet Mexican breeze blew in my face.

The Stay

We dropped our stuff in the rental car. Mom took me to a bunch of different landmarks and taught me about Mexican agriculture. Then we finally got to the beach. It was pretty crowded and basically covered in sun umbrellas. I grabbed my towel and rolled it out on the sand in a spot free from people. When I went to the water, I stuck my head under the water and grabbed a handful of seashells. I looked back at my towel and noticed it wasn't there. I saw Simon giggling a few feet away dangling my towel over the water. I grabbed his pail, filled it with water, and dumped water over his head. I finally got my towel from him and dried myself off. I looked around, and seeing all of this water made me need to use the bathroom. I don't like to use the ocean—that is too much like Simon—so I went up to Grams and said, "*Baño*" ("Bathroom"), and we went up to the bathroom. It felt like a hike with all of the sand delaying our running.

"*¡Vamos!*" she said. I ran without opening my legs.

When I finally reached the restroom, there was a line *miles* long! (Maybe not so long, but still.) It looked like a long swim class lining up for a restroom break, and we were the ones who were late to class *and* last in line. It took like twenty minutes for the line to be down to the last few people. At this point I was considering the ocean, but if I moved, our spot would be taken. There were only two stalls in the restroom, and that ticked me off. How was this a public beach bathroom and they only had two stalls?! The lady in front of us had like eight children, two of whom were boys, which disgusted me. When all of them finally got out, the boys were giggling and laughing.

"Girls are icky," one of them said.

"Yeah, they're nasty," the other one agreed. I guess they were on vacation too, since they weren't speaking Spanish.

When we entered the bathroom, I was underwhelmed. Toilet paper was on the floor, scattered everywhere, and someone sat their flip-flop under the dryer so it was noisy. I went into the small stall, and Grams went into the big one that was meant for older people. *"Ay ay ay, caramba!"* she said when she got inside.

"What?" I asked.

"¡Hay un bicho!" ("There's a bug!") she squealed.

I looked at my toilet, and it was bug-free. I rushed to get out of there because who knows what Simon was doing to my towel while I was in there. (It was probably soaked in ocean water—or something else—yuck!) With as bad as things were going so far, I felt relieved that I was here.

I walked out of the bathroom, and the sand was BURNING HOT! "Ahhhhh! *¡La arena está tan caliente!*" ("The sand is so hot!") I just said a full sentence in Spanish! Wow! "Did you hear that, Grams? I said a full sentence in Spanish!" But I couldn't wait for her to answer. I saw the boy who'd called girls icky touching my towel with his hands. *And* he was in the water! The sand was practically melting my toes off. I started a full-on run. By the time I slowed my run, I was knee deep in the water, and the boy didn't see me until I was two feet away from him.

He side-stepped me, and I dropped my

towel. I went belly-flopping into the water. "*Owwwwww.*" And then it went dark. Everything was clouded. I think I was underwater. I couldn't move, but at least my toes felt better. I heard a loud whistle, and within three seconds I was being dragged out of the water.

"*Jovencita, ¿estás bien?*" ("Little girl, are you okay?")

I'd been holding my breath until the lifeguard pulled me out.

"*Sí,*" I said. I'd never seen Grams run

before, but now she looked like a track star. I asked what had happened and he basically explained that I fell in the water and I was just a little shaken.

"*Vamos a la casa de tu tío*" ("Let's go to your uncle's house"), my mom said. Grams was panting when she reached me. Her feet were red, and she was sweating. "*¿Qué te ha pasado?*" ("What happened to you?"), said Mom.

"I was running."

She started to walk back to the rental car. Dad pulled out the keys.

Mom looked at Simon, and he sighed. "I am sorry that you belly-flopped into the ocean." He started to giggle at the word *belly-flop*. "And that I took your towel."

"I accept your (fake) apology," I said, rolling my eyes.

When we got to Tío Mateo's house, I was surprised, and so was Grams, because the sight of it made her gasp. "Oh, *vaya*" ("Oh, wow"), she said. The outside was white with big windows that were outlined with gold. The front doors were the size of my house! It looked like the white house with a driveway made of marvel stone.

"This is MATEO'S?" asked Mom.

"It seems as if it is," said my dad.

"Well, are we going in or not?" I asked. Simon was already ringing the doorbell for the thirty-third time. When we all caught up to him, a lady opened the door. Grams, Mom, Dad, Simon, and I were all shocked at the sight of her. She was a Mexican lady with long, black hair that went down to her back. She wore a romper that was very short, and it was a silky gold color. She had on a blindingly bright lip gloss.

"*Hola.*"

She was so graceful when she spoke that my mom had to catch her breath. "Oh. *Hola, estamos aquí por Mateo.*" ("Oh. Hello, we are here for Mateo"), Mom said, testing her. The lady smiled and motioned us inside. All of the furniture was a baby blue color made with velvet fabric with white carpets and shiny things hanging from the ceiling.

"*Mi amor, tenemos visitantes*" ("My love, we have visitors"), she called.

Tío Mateo came down the three rows of stairs in another one of his "*originales lujosas,*" but this one was a peach color instead of that crazy green.

"¡Hola, Tío Mateo!" Simon and I said at the same time. He opened his arms and we came running in.

"*Hola*, my little princess and prince! You have grown since the last time I've seen you." Once we pulled away, my mom and Grams gave him hugs. When finally my dad came, they did something I didn't even understand:

"Hey man!" said Dad.

"What's up, dog?" replied Tío.

"Nothing man, how about you, thun?"

"Psh, you know how it is."

Once we were done saying our hellos, the lady came in and locked arms with him. "Oh! My wife. Valentina." She waved and kissed him on the cheek.

"You had a wedding without us?" I asked.

"No, Harper, no. I just didn't want to draw you out here just for a day of champagne and cake." He offended me so much, but it looked like he hurt Simon's feelings more. "Tío Mateo, I like cake..." Simon started to cry. What a first impression.

"*Vamos*, Simon, we can get you all cleaned up." My mom and Grams led Simon up the stairs. I saw Mom steal a glance at Tío Mateo.

"Uh, Harper, here, why don't you talk with your uncle? I'll go put your bags away," said my dad as he started up the stairs.

"So you must be Harper," Valentina said.

"*Sí.*" I decided to try to speak as much Spanish as possible in Mexico, just because that's what most people here spoke.

"So how is middle school, *niña*?" she said.

"*Bien. No soy lo que llamarías estudiante de estrella*" ("Fine, I'm not what you would call a star student"). I was really catching on!

"*Bien, bien.*" Even though she was asking me questions, it didn't seem like she cared about my answers.

***

"You should get ready for bed," Grams told me after we had enchiladas for dinner.

"Okay." I went up to the room that had my suitcases in front of it. When I opened the door there was a bed five times as big as mine. The room itself was amazing—it had yellow walls, a portrait of a puppy, and red sheets. I plopped on the bed and immediately fell in love. "Oh, my," I said in awe. I put on my orange T-shirt with a dinosaur in the middle. I went into the living room to see Tío Mateo and Mom arguing.

"You can't be having a wife that dresses

inappropriately in front of my children!" she said.

"How can you tell me who I can and can't marry, Elena?" he said.

"Mateo!" She lowered to a whisper. "You are acting like you were with your last wife. You have to make the right decisions, *hermano*, you have to! And we all know this is her property. If you two don't work, then you're back out in the real world finding a job and another place to live in."

He seemed offended. "Why do you have to be in my life so much, Elena? Why?" he asked.

"I am going to KEEP being in your life, Mateo! And as you fall, I help you get back up. So if I'm not in your life, then you will stay on the ground!" She started to get *mad* mad. So mad her face went plain. "I will NOT be a part of this. My family will leave, *hermano*, and you will be here with your wife." My mom went down the hall.

After I was sure she was gone, I walked

in the kitchen all casual-like and pretended to be getting a glass of water. *"Hola, Tío Mateo,"* I said. He looked sick to his stomach.

"¿Qué haces aquí tan tarde?" ("What are you doing out here so late?)

"Uh, just getting some *agua*. What are you doing?"

"Just, uh...taking a few moments to get sleepy."

Yeah, right!

The next morning my mom was cherry-red, and she barged into my room at 7:30 am.

"Vamos. Let's go. We're leaving."

"Mami, but—" She put her hand up.

"Harper. I said *vamos,* we are leaving RIGHT NOW, so pack your bags."

And just like that, she left me in my room. Mom and Dad got a hotel room online at a place called *El Paraíso.* The hotel had a pool and hot tub for only people who had a room card. I was excited to show off my other bathing suit because I got it at the end of summer last year, so I hadn't gotten to wear it yet. Grams got her own hotel room, so I didn't see her often. Simon went right to the hot tub, so I went to the pool.

I asked Mom if we could get room service when we got back to the hotel room, but she said the same thing: "Do you see me begging my mami to work extra?"

Blah, blah, blah. I examined the place: big pool, not too crowded, the perfect vacation place if you ask me. In the corner there was an iPad that had a digital map of the hotel with things you could do. I looked at the things-to-do section and searched for *something*. The only thing that felt right was a job. This vacation was supposed to be relaxing, but my parents just spent a whole bunch of money on a trip that only happened because I lied to my mom about why I wanted to go here. I had to have something to keep my mind off that. And just relaxing was reminding me more of how I could be getting ready for school in two days, not on a fake Mexican-ancestor-learning trip.

I found a snack-bar job that was right in front of the pool. It was a buffet, so all I had to do was charge a one-time fee and make sure no one stole food without a card. I decided to ask Grams, but I had to find her hotel room; luckily, this resort wasn't too big and I found her within ten minutes.

"Grams, I know this is a vacation, and I'm supposed to have fun and enjoy myself and bask in the Mexican sun and- well, you get the gist- but, what I'm trying to ask is can I get a job?" I was afraid I would have to explain why I want a job during vacation, but she said I could apply for the job.

When I walked in the buffet, I saw a lady in a green sundress and brown sandals, with the same color brown hair and very tanned skin. She wore rings on every finger, but they were all the same, and she had different colored nails. Blue, green, yellow, blue, green, yellow. She motioned to the door, and we interviewed by the pool in a cabana.

"So why do you want to work here?"

"I want to work here because I need a job, and I am highly responsible."

And it went on for another hour or so and ended with, "Thank you so much. I'll call you if you make the cut."

As far as I could see, I got the job. Not only did I flash my charming smile, but I also didn't see anyone come for any interviews after I spied on the place for an hour. So I got a brand new outfit from the gift shop. I got purple tights, light blue shorts, and a white tank top with a sunrise on it. I also got these cool sandals that were white with sparkly buckles.

I got a call from the snack bar and they said I got the job (I kinda already knew that, but I didn't brag). I went through the door that said, "EMPLOYEES ONLY" and got to work.

This job wasn't hard at all. The only challenge was this old man who was probably senile who thought he was at his old job as a chef and tried to get into the kitchen.

"Onion up! Little girl, get out of my kitchen!" he told me. I had to get help from the boss to handle this.

***

When I went up to the hotel, Mom wasn't there; it was just Simon, Dad, and Grams. "Where's Mom?" I asked.

"I—I don't know," Dad said, concerned.

Simon had tears in his eyes, and he was looking under the bed. "Mami, Mami, where are you?" he said.

Grams and Dad were looking out the window hoping to see her. "She went out in the hall to use the bathroom but never came back," Dad said to himself.

I went down to the pool and asked the

lifeguard. "Excuse me, miss?" She had a red bathing suit and short-cropped blond hair.

"Yes sweetie?" she asked.

"Um, have you seen a lady with brown, curly hair, deep hazel eyes?" The lady shook her head. I sprinted down to the main office.

"Um, do you recall a lady exiting here?"

"No," he said plainly. "Also, there are lots of women here."

"Can you look up the name Elena Ellison?"

He sighed and clicked on his computer. "Um...there has been no guest named Elena Ellison in the past three months." And he went back to looking at paperwork. I started to cry.

"Dad, they haven't had a person named Elena for three months!" My dad was putting on his shoes. "Ok. All right. We're going to search Mexico. Harper put on your shoes."

Simon sat in his bed and half put on his shoes and half cried. It was hard for me to hold myself back from crying even harder. We checked everywhere, even Tío Mateo's house. Grams got tired of walking all over the beaches and resorts, so we left her at Tío's house, but I could tell she didn't want to quit looking. We kept looking but didn't find her anywhere. We checked the airport and *so* many other places. We booked the hotel for another week or so, and I continued to work just to keep my mind off the fact that this is all my fault. My dad wasn't giving up though, so neither was I.

"Come on. We will search the far side of the beach first," he said. Although he'd said that five times in the past week, I went along with it. We spent all day looking and we didn't find anything.

"Dad, I think we may need professionals to do the job. I mean people who can go all over in double the time," Simon said.

Then it hit me. "Dad, I'm missing school!" I said once we reached the hotel room.

"Oh, my." He started pacing; for a minute I felt like I shouldn't have told him. He was already under a lot of stress. I mean, we'd been having takeout for dinner for the past few days.

"Uh, I mean, it's fine. The principal announced that, well, um—he said that we have an early spring break," I lied. It was not even close to spring break, but he was so distracted he wouldn't notice.

"Oh. Well, that clears things up. I'll be on the phone with the police," he said. I was right.

The next morning, we booked the same hotel room. Dad was slumping in a chair eating cheese balls and drinking soda. I decided not to ask why he was in a bathrobe and one flip-flop. Simon was playing cars silently in the corner. I got ready for work early. I didn't know if they would still let me work there since I'd been leaving early so often to look for Mom, but I wanted to get out of this hotel room. Maybe I could scan the resort for the millionth time.

"Simon, let's go," I said. He looked me up and down.

"Why would *you* want to take *me* somewhere?" he asked suspiciously. I pointed to Dad and he started putting on his shoes.

When we got to the snack bar, Simon ran to the pool, and as I walked in, I noticed there was a new employee. Oh no, did they replace me? As I got closer, I saw her name tag. Her name was Savannah. She wore black ripped jeans and an orange off-the-shoulders shirt with a loose belt.

"Hey," I said.

"Hi, um, the boss needs me to show you the new schedule," Savannah said. She took me behind the door, and into the back room where we refill the snacks and then sprayed me with this minty-leaf-smelling stuff. I felt woozy and fell down.

Spy Place

I woke up in a weird facility that looked the size of a football field. The walls were black and had huge pictures of people with mustaches. It also had this weird stuff there that was labeled with things like, "Mind Eraser Ray Gun." It was weird. I saw Savannah. She was talking to this really tall guy in black. I heard her saying something; I think she was saying, "She was onto me." I didn't know why she said that. The only reason I was onto her now was because she kidnapped me. The tall guy spoke in a gruff voice and he said something like, "As long as she's here, you know where to take her. The other side will be looking for her I'm sure." I looked around and noticed I was in a bag, a big brown bag that had little holes. Savannah picked me up and set me down somewhere small and cramped. I tried to get my phone out, and when I did, there was no Wi-Fi, and it died right when I turned it on.

When I thought she had left, I moved around and got a rip in the bag. The rip was so small I had to squeeze my stomach in to get out.

"Ugh," I said. I was still feeling woozy. "What?" I was in a small room with all-white walls and a couch that was at least ten years old. The room smelled like dust bunnies and heat. I don't know if it's possible to smell heat, but it smelled hot. Probably because there were no windows. A clinking sound like locks being unlocked came from behind the metal door by the couch. Savannah walked in with a chair.

She slammed it down and said, "Hello, Harper," like we were resuming a good conversation and she didn't just trap me in a room. "Sorry about the spray. It was mandatory." She didn't sound sorry.

"Uh..." I started.

"Save it, Harper. We have to move you somewhere," she said, taking the friendliness out of her voice.

"We?" Once I asked, she glared at me with a mixture of disgust and sympathy.

"You don't need to worry about that yet." She grabbed me by the arm and basically dragged me down the long halls of black and white. We stopped at a large metal door that smelled like gas. "When we enter here, don't speak," she said.

"EXCUSE ME??!!" I said.

"Yeah, okay, get it ALL out now before we enter, sounds good. You done yet?" she asked.

"AHHHHHHHHHHH!" I screamed.

"Okay now? All right," Savannah said as she slapped a piece of tape over my mouth. "So this is what you need to know. This is a place where we will train you to become a spy. Your m- uh, *you* are wanted. So we want to *protect* you from the other side—a group of terrible people—we don't know their plan, but we do know they want to take over the spy industries all over the world." *oh wow- what is this some kind of superhero TV show?* I thought. She opened the door and I saw all the people with mustaches sitting at a big table.

"*Ciao.* Thank you, Savannah, for bringing us this boring young lady. You can put her in the corner, and we'll get to the questions," one said, but then the others started talking. They were speaking in what sounded like Italian, so I could not understand them.

"*Sì, va bene, spie*" ("Yeah, all right, spies"), Savannah said, handing me a black thing. She pointed at her ear, so I put it in my ear.

"Now that you can understand us...WHY ARE YOU HERE AND WHAT IS YOUR MOTIVE?" the mustache crew said. I could understand them with the earpiece now. Their yelling scared me a bit, but I'd watched movies and I knew what to do. "Here due to a vacation. Motive: None," I said. It came out in Italian. "YEAH, RIGHT! Death penalty! Take her to the—"

"No, wait! There must be some way that I can take something other than...that." I said.

"Well," they said, "I guess you are here for a reason, so you will be a spy."

"That, or...die?"

"Yes," they said. They looked pretty satisfied with me dying. I looked down, considering my two horrible choices.

"I—I will be a spy." I frowned.

"Time for training!" One of the guys snapped his fingers, and immediately a lady came through the door, as if waiting for me.

"*Dai.*" I followed her through long, long hallways and stairs until we reached a dead end.

"Umm, excuse me, lady? We may have taken a wrong tu—" I started. But she put her hand up and shushed me. Then she did the weirdest thing. She put her hand on the wall, and it opened into a small room with brown walls, one chair, and a desk; the only light was hanging in the middle of the room. She pushed me in, and the magic wall closed. Out of nowhere, Savannah was standing in the corner in a whole different outfit. It was blue workout tights with black stripes and a black silk crop top with blue stripes.

"Here." She handed me a red workout outfit with green stripes.

"Uh...thanks?" I said. "Who were those guys?" I asked.

"The deciding council. They decide on the most important things that boss doesn't decide on. Like whether to kill you or let you become a spy. Now get dressed, there is too much to explain in so little time." But she stayed in the room.

"Are you going to leave me to get dressed?" I asked.

"Oh. right." She only put on sunglasses.

"HELLO??" I yelled. I was starting to think she couldn't process words. "Savannah?" I said urgingly.

"HARPER! I can't see you using these glasses," she said, like I should understand that.

"Are those sunglasses magic, too?" I murmured.

"Magic? What in the world?" She looked at me crazily, like I should know this stuff.

"Yeah. Magic." I told her.

"These aren't magic," she said matter-of-factly.

"So you've been lying about how you can't see me?" I gasped.

"No. I haven't," she said, annoyed.

"Then—ugh, turn around, still," I finally said. Once I changed my clothes we were on our way upstairs.

"Magic isn't a thing here, Harper," she said.

"What do you mean?" I asked.

"Well, instead of magic, it's skill," she told me.

"If it's skill, then how can you explain those?" I asked.

"Tech," Savannah told me.

"Tech?"

"Yep. Tech," she repeated.

"Where am I, anyway?" I changed the subject.

"The YSAOE," Savannah answered.

"The what?" I asked.

"The Youth Spy Agency of Experts," she said, irritated.

"So are you one of them?" I asked.

"You ask lots of questions. I hope they break you," she said.

"Break me?" I practically shouted.

"Yes. Get you to be a real spy, y'know...act like one."

"Pardon me?" I asked.

"You heard me," Savannah said.

"So how did they break you?"

She stopped and sighed. I just realized I was sweating and still on the steps.

"Well...work. Hard, hard work. Spies are complicated, in a way you wouldn't understand. This is not like learning variables. It's a life or death job and death is an inch away from you all the time when you're a spy. Don't play around." We went up about five more flights of steps until we spoke to each other again.

"The top is only a few flights away," she said. After a few flights, we were at a door totally covered in black paper. When we walked in, I saw all types of people. Each person was doing a different thing. I saw a boy beating up a dummy on a stand, a girl mixing two beakers of bubbly red-and-yellow potion stuff, two people doing good cop/bad cop, and so many other things.

"Take a seat." Savannah pointed to a chair across the room.

"Um, I don't know if you noticed, but that chair happens to be guarded by people who look like they want to punch me," I responded.

"Oh, I know," she said. "This is gonna be *good*," I heard her mumble.

"Hey look, a giant donut!" I said, trying to distract the people. Their stare at me got even deeper after I said that.

"Loosen up!" Savannah said to me, but I couldn't. I was super stiff, and I was freaking out. "These are always the hardest ones to break," Savannah huffed.

"You're not breaking me!" I said.

"And why not?" she asked.

"Because! Because you're not," I tried to explain.

"'Because' is not a reason, Harper!" she yelled.

"Just stop!" I called out. I dropped down to the floor. I missed my family, even Simon.

Savannah got a sympathetic look on her face. "Sorry," she started. "I—I didn't mean to." She looked down at the floor. She put her hand out to help me up. When she looked up, her face was as solid as before.

"No thanks." I got up by myself.

"What? I'm just trying to help you," she said, although she didn't sound like she was trying to help. "Whatever." Savannah rolled her eyes. "Sit back down in the chair, this will only take a moment."

I hesitated, but I sat.

"George," she said, and then a teenager came in: maybe tenth grade, high tops, dark skin, muscly but humanlike.

"So. You're Harper. Daughter of Elena Ellison. Right?" He sounded like a grown man.

"Y-yes. Who wants to know?" I asked.

"George Howard," he said, sticking out his hand. I just shook my head.

"Okay. This is the one who has the breaking fear," Savannah said. "Oh, so you're afraid of spying?" George asked. Yet again I nodded. "Your mom was a spy. *Kinda*," he said.

Mom? Where's mom? How does he know her? And what does she have to do with any of this? SPY? Questions raced through my head. But only one question tugged in the back of my head. I spoke, "What do you mean, *kinda*?"

"I mean what I say," he said. He took that more seriously than I thought he would. He exhaled. "I mean what I say, and I say what I mean. It has always been like that, and that won't ever change." He seemed to be talking more to himself than me.

"So my mom was 'kinda' a spy?" I asked.

"Yes. A 'kinda' spy." Savannah cleared her throat.

"But let's get to the main reason I am here," said George. "I am your 'counselor.'" He put "counselor" in quotations.

"Why do you put 'counselor' in quotations?"

"Because an actual counselor is basically in charge of you. But I'm not."

"So what do you do as my 'counselor'?" I asked.

"I will report to you about what needs to be done," he said.

"Report from whom?" I asked.

"The boss, of course." he said, snarkily.

"Who's the boss?" I asked.

"Not me," he said, as if he wanted to be.

"Then who is?" I asked.

"Uh..." He looked at Savannah as if pleading for her to step in.

"The boss is the person we all work for, Harper. The main source—as far as we know—so we need you here to be the best spy you can be," Savannah said.

"But why me?" I asked.

"Because of your mother," George stepped back in.

"What does my mo—" I started, but then a booming voice echoed through the room.

"Trainees!" It was so loud I stumbled out of my chair. George stood up straighter, making him look older. Savannah straightened her shirt and brushed back her hair. Everyone around me was standing in a straight line, shoulder to shoulder. When I got up, the loud voice was towering over me. The sight of him made me breathless. "P-p-principal Kaleb?" How is my school principal here? He should be at school. Although if he works here that would explain why he's always off campus.

He wore a strange running outfit, and he'd gotten a line up on his hairline. His emotion didn't even change. His mouth was a straight line.

"Line!" he boomed.

I thought he said "lime," so I didn't move, just grimaced. He glared at George, and George immediately pulled me from the ground and took me to the end of the line.

"Don't get on the bad side of him," George warned before fixing his face from a worried frown to an upturned business face. Savannah was still in her place, staring straight at the wall.

"Sir," she said.

"Attend motion!" he bellowed.

Savannah and George stepped back, and everyone in my line stepped forward, so I followed.

"Janice Fame!" A girl in a purple workout suit stepped up. "Here and ready to take 'em." She cracked her knuckles so hard I thought her fingers would dislocate.

"Daron Baxtor!" A small snaggle toothed boy, maybe six, stepped up. "Here and ready to break 'em."

Principal Kaleb pointed to me. "That's

her, little man." Daron walked up to me.

"Hewo, Harper. I will be bweaking you." He sounded so small and innocent, I didn't want to tell him that he was funny. I couldn't help it, though. I broke out into laughter.

I was laughing so hard I teared up a bit. Then little Daron punched me in the stomach so hard that I thought an enchilada would come out.

"O—" I didn't even remember the term. "O—is it oy or ow?" I asked.

"Ow. The term is Ow. It'll come back to you," Daron said.

"OW," I repeated.

Principal Kaleb pinched the bridge of his nose. "Infirmary." A boy came and motioned me down the halls until I reached a big room filled with people.

Either my vision was getting fuzzy or one of the patients had a bird sitting next to them. I sat on the bed and lay down. A nurse with a name tag that said "Tiffany" came up to me and examined my stomach.

"Hmmm...London!"

Another girl came in and said, "Pick 443918! James!"

Another boy came in, and he was holding a needle practically two yards long and pointing it at my stomach.

"WOW!" I yelled. "Hold it right there, mister!" I jumped up and winced at the pain of my stomach.

"It's okay, Harper. Just sit still." I laid

down, and the next thing I knew I was asleep. Then I woke up. It was dark outside and the other people in the rooms were whispering to each other. I woozily looked at them.

"You...you have a bird on your head." Then they started giggling again. I had to get out of this place. I opened the window. "If you don't tell anybody, I'll give you a lollipop from my house!" I told them. They looked at me like I was insane.

"We aren't little kids. A lollipop is like this to us." She grabbed a water bottle and crushed it.

"Yeah. Ditto, so uh, I'll pay you each ten bucks. *Please?*"

"Look, clearly you don't have any good offers. We dare you to do something crazy!" they said angrily.

"But...okay," I agreed. I pushed at the window, but it didn't move. I pushed it up and it slid open. Cold air hit my face. I reached my leg out the window thinking I would get electrocuted or something, but I didn't, so I got out the window all the way. "Here goes something crazy. I'm escaping."

I looked around. This was a pretty big field: grassy, had a few bushes here and there, and—a fence! It was only two feet high so I jumped over it—kinda. It was electric, and I fell over, stunned. The cold grass gently cushioned me as I was sent off to sleep, but not soon enough, because those kids went laughing their heads off.

When I could feel my eyelids, I looked up and saw Principal Kaleb leaning over me with a flashlight. I was in big trouble.

"Harper Rosa Gina Luna Louise Ellison! What in the world were you thinking?"

I'd never heard anyone say my full name except for my mom when I was at the water park and I left Simon by himself to go play with other kids and he ended up playing with high schoolers that were jumping off the top of the slides instead of sliding down them, and so Simon tried it—it's a long story. "Um, it's not 'Louise,'" I corrected him.

"Excuse me?"

"Yes. It's not '*Louise*,' it's *Larisa*. And how do you know my full name?"

"However. JUMPING OVER THE GATE? HAVE YOU LOST YOUR MIND??" he yelled once I was able to stand.

"Principal Kaleb, you can't yell at me. I barely know you."

"Excuse me?"

"I don't know you. So in the end, you can't yell at me," I said. "Or do I need to repeat myself, *grandpa*?" He blinked. I just kept on going. "Can someone turn on your hearing aid?" I asked.

He looked like he was about to scream his head off. Then I noticed a girl standing by the door. She ducked and ran before Principal Kaleb could spot her, but she was too late. He turned around and started to run towards her. Like *fast*. His tie was blowing in the wind towards his face. His flashlight fell out of his hands. I couldn't tell who the girl was that he was running after. I saw he dropped a remote—that's all that was there. It had two buttons: a lightning bolt and a lightning bolt with a big X over it. I clicked the one with the X over it. Nothing happened for a split second, then the whole gate started vibrating and blue electricity started coming out of it. It was blinding and loud. I thought that someone was going to hear me and take me back into that circus of killing machines, but no one did. I guess this field was so big the spy people could barely hear anything. The gate stopped shooting electricity out, and the ground stopped shaking. Then the gate vanished.

"Totally magic," I whispered.

"Hey!" a faint voice shouted.

"Huh?" I looked side to side.

"Hey!" it repeated.

Then a girl knocked into me from behind. I was dizzy for a minute, shaken a little. Two legs, check. Both arms, check. Neck intact, check. Hair still on my head, check. My hair was very knotted and frizzing everywhere. That electricity must've made my hair stick up.

"GET INSIDE!" Principal Kaleb screamed. I remembered what George had told me: *"Don't get on the bad side of him"* I already had. He helped me and the girl up and dragged us through the grassy field. While we were being dragged, I got a glimpse of the girl. She was pale and thin. She was blonde and wore a big green sweater and black leggings. Her blonde hair had a streak of black in it, she had light pink lip gloss, and she was sweating like she had been running for a long time. Principal Kaleb took us into the auditorium and sat us in cold metal chairs. There was a long steel table in front of us and one chair across from us.

I thought this was an interrogation. The

girl looked down at her beaten-up shoes and up at me with a hopeful look. Principal Kaleb yanked the chair across from us and sat down. And with a snap of his fingers, the room was pitch black. Screeching sounds were made around me, and then one light popped on; it was a dim yellow and the only thing we could see was Principal Kaleb's face.

"Harper. Care to explain to me why you were out by the fence in the field?"

"No."

"Harper. Lives are on the line."

"Whose lives?"

"None of your business right now."

"I am not giving any information to a stranger."

"We aren't playing this game today, Harper."

"Fine, I was escaping."

"Why?"

"Because."

"Because why?"

"Because I don't like it here."

"Why not?"

"BECAUSE I DON'T!!"

"That's not an answer."

"I don't like it here because I was kidnapped by this random girl, no one is telling me why I'm here, my family is back in Mexico probably crying their eyes out, my mom is missing, Umma is back home in Washington, Raymond—" I stopped myself.

"Who's Raymond?" He asked.

"No one." He kept asking me for twenty minutes, but soon, he knew I wasn't going to budge.

"Willow. Care to explain why you were spying on us in the field?"

"This *is* a spying academy, isn't it?"

"Yes. But you are not here to get into stuff you don't need to get into."

"That's what spies do."

At this point, she had him puzzled. After five minutes of trying to figure out how she just tricked him, he went back to interrogating. "Well not *you*."

"Why not *me*?" she asked.

"Because you aren't that kind of spy."

"So what kinda spy am I?"

"A different spy."

"And why is that?"

"Because...I don't *feel* like properly answering."

"I don't either, then."

"Oh will you both just shut u—I mean... SHHHHH!" I said, breaking up their argument. I was loud. Both of them turned their faces towards me, red with anger. "Okay, okay! Go back to arguing!"

"Oh, you do!"

"Nuh-uh!"

"Uh-huh!"

It went on like this for a few minutes. I thought about breaking out again, but it was too risky of another stare-down. I reached across the table and snatched Principal

Kaleb's phone. He didn't have a password on his phone, fortunately. I punched in Chrissy's number and texted her.

Me: Hey it's me Harper. :D

Chris: Harper? What happened to ur old number?

Me: I got kidnapped

Chris: :O :O :O :O

Me: Yea

Me: This is someone else's phone...I will not specify who.

Chris: Who is it?

Me: NO ONE!

Chris: Send me ur location, my dad can track you.

Me: kk

Chris: Lemme tell my dad

Me: I can't find it D:

Chris: Go to location then do send

Me: Oh I see it

Me: Adam Kaleb's location sent

Me: Oops, that auto typed

Chris: Principal Kaleb kidnapped you!?!?

Chris: HELLO? YOU THERE HARPER

Then I was caught.

"Harper! What are you doing?" Principal Kaleb asked, red in the face with anger.

"I can explain—"

"Not this time Harper!" He snatched his phone and typed something. He took me to a hallway, and I wondered what he did to Willow. I walked up these stairs.

Then he pulled me to a room with Savannah. It had burgundy walls and two twin beds. Both of them had white sheets, comforters, and pillows. A small cream-colored nightstand stood in the middle of the twin beds. A door that led probably to the bathroom stood in the corner. Other than that, and a window over the night stand, the room was pretty boring.

"This is your new *dorm room!*" he said. "TALK." He pointed to Savannah, who yanked me back and smiled at Principal Kaleb. She shut the door and gave me a glare so angry that it sent a chill down my spine.

"I go on one short mission and I come back to this?" She didn't even let me answer.

"Look. You can't fool around in this program. You have to want to have it."

"Have what?" She just stood there giving me the side-eye.

"I can't fail at being your supervisor. You put me at risk, and I can't afford that. So just try your best and stay out of trouble."

"What is Principal Kaleb doing here?"

"Principal Kaleb? You mean Coach Kaleb? He's been the spy company's key negotiator, fitness director, and assignment director for about three years. Once associated with the 'other side' but is now working for us," she answered angrily. The *Other Side?* Everyone kept talking about that. And that was all of the talking we did for the night. The only sound was her muttering to herself and taking deep breaths. I could barely sleep, though. I thought about attempting to escape, but I knew they saw the gate was gone, so they'd probably fixed it.

But just for good measures, I looked out of the window. The gate was still there, but something was different about it. Suddenly I had the urge to go out there. I tried to open the window, but it was sealed shut. I looked at the vent, and it had nails keeping it in place.

So I tiptoed out of the room. The door didn't squeak at all, but I only opened it a crack, not taking any chances. Once I reached the back door that now had a fingerprint recognition device instead of a doorknob, I thought I was busted, but it looked like someone had already cracked the case. The door was already open. I stepped in, and the wind blew through my hair. My feet were getting cold on the grass. I got to the gate and saw that the person who was already out there was Willow.

Willow and a Punch

"**W**hat are you doing out here?" I asked Willow.

"Nothing."

"I mean, you're doing *something*."

"Yes...but nothing that you should know about." She crossed her arms.

"Why?"

"'Cause."

"'Cause what?" I put my hands on my hips.

"Eh, I wanted to?"

"And why did you want to?"

"SPY REASONS."

"Are you afraid of breaking, too?" I asked.

"Um...exactly! Yep. So why don't you just, ya know, *leave*, and yeah, we'll both face our fears of *breaking* out."

"That's not what breaking is."

"Of course it isn't...um, yeah, just go, would you?"

"No—no, I will not."

"Whyyyyy? Please!"

"Fine."

I lied. I snuck behind a bush by the door and listened to her.

"The people here are *stupid*," she said in a snootier tone than usual. "This one girl actually just left! I was being *so* suspicious, she's so gullible." I almost threw up my hands. How rude, I thought.

"JEEZ! So soon!" I couldn't hear the person she was talking to, so I guessed she was on the phone. "Okay, fine." And she stopped talking, so I'm guessing she hung up.

She crept around the building and put a

device on the wall. It expanded and built up into a ladder so tall it reached the top of the roof. She started climbing it, and when she reached the top she looked around, then put out another device. I followed her and got a glimpse of the device. It was a small, shiny, circular, black object, and it had two purple lines glowing on the sides. The lines opened up, and the roof turned purple.

I looked at it and noticed it was liquid. "This is why you would make a great spy." Savannah was behind me. She startled me, and I had a little inner shriek.

"I'm *not* spying. I'm...*eavesdropping*."

"Oh, yeah. *Huge* difference," Savannah said *super* sarcastically.

I turned around, and there she was. Willow was standing right next to me, holding a gadget to my back. Savannah went into action and held a gadget pointing at Willow. It was silent. Everyone was standing *completely* still. I stepped to the side, and

Willow pulled her gadget's trigger. I closed my eyes. Nothing happened.

Savannah half-smiled. "Lookin' for this?" She held up a small, square chip that was about two millimeters thick and had a faint purple glow. Savannah and Willow had a fistfight.

Willow punched Savannah in the leg. Then Savannah came back with punches to Willow's knee and head. Willow kicked Savannah and flipped her over, then Savannah came with a save as she pulled Willow down with her. Willow rolled away. Savannah caught her wrist, pulled her, and flipped her over. Willow kicked Savannah in the ankles, which made Savannah fall to the floor. Willow pulled Savannah's hair. Then suddenly Savannah somersaulted up, grabbed Willow, and tried to throw her off of the roof. But Willow held onto Savannah and flipped her off the building. Savannah fell all the way off the roof.

Willow brushed her shoulder. I knew I needed to do something. I grabbed Willow off guard: I jumped off the roof.

Willow fell along with me, and Savannah was holding on to the ladder by a finger. I was glad that she could move; her hands were bruised and scratched up like they had been dragged along the wall. Then she dropped.

At that *exact* moment, George walked out. "What in the *world?*" he asked. "What is going on here?" He pressed a red button on the wall.

Savannah reached her hand up. In a way, she protested him pushing it. He tried to approach, but Willow rolled over to him and clicked a button on her gadget, and he fell backward. She grabbed him by the leg and set him down beside the building. Immediately Kaleb (HA! I am calling him KALEB from now on!) came rushing over. He was hopping mad. Literally, he was jumping up and down. I pulled Savannah by the wrist and we tried to make a run for it. We were bruised so badly that we limped to a bush. I saw Savannah had a bad cut on her knee.

"Hey. Your knee is gushing out blood," I pointed out. She looked grim and sweaty with a scratch across her head. She breathed heavily as if she were trying to keep herself from fainting. "I'm...fine," she said between gasps. I saw Willow out of the corner of my eye.

She was crawling weakly across the field to Kaleb. "Mr. Kaleb! Please! Harper told me that she wanted to show me a surprise, but she took me up the roof! I think she got a hold of your body booster, and then she threw me off the roof!" She started to cry. Part of me was saying, *"SHE IS A LIAR!!!!! You shouldn't believe her! Just tell her off!"* And the other said, *"Awwwww! You should go and help her up."* I didn't come out of the bush because either way, I had something to do with this, and wasn't selling myself out now.

I looked back to Savannah, and she was lying on the ground with her eyes closed. I couldn't tell if she was asleep or unconscious. I picked her up and hoisted her over my shoulders.

I heard Kaleb tell Willow, "Oh, I knew it from the beginning. Harper is a violent anti-spy out to get us." That triggered me.

I crawled out the bush and yelled at him, "WHAT THE HECK IS AN ANTI-SPY, AND WOULD I SAVE SAVANNAH FROM WILLOW IF I WERE A VIOLENT ANTI-SPY?!"

Kaleb pulled out the gadget Willow had earlier and tased me. I fell to the ground. All I felt was the cold grass brushing over me for a second, then I could feel warm rubber. After that I felt cool cement.

I'm Breaking You Out

I woke up in a cell. There was a TV in the corner playing a slideshow.

"You are an ANTI-SPY! Bad thing for you, we know how to contain you!" it said in a cheerful voice as the screen showed a spy in chains.

"Anyway, you will eat twice a day, sleep for thirteen hours, and watch these slides for the rest of your life! Sounds like quite the guilt tri—" it got cut off by Kaleb on the screen.

"Hello, anti-spies and others that are being contained." He wiped his eyes. "Anyway, this is just my way of saying.... YOU LOSE!!"

He stuck out his tongue, and the video resumed: "—p, huh? Well, it is." Then the video repeated.

Right when I was going to turn off the TV, somehow Savannah came in. "Come on,

I'm breaking you out," she said.

"What do you mean, 'breaking me out'?" I said. She started to take a gadget out of her pocket. "What is that?" She took the cap off and told me to stand back. Then she zapped the door open.

"The guards are out cold. But they'll wake up soon. We should get moving," she said as she cleared smoke from her eyes.

"Yeah, sure," I said, stepping over the half broken and half-melted cell door. We walked past the guards and snuck around the place, dodging people and guards until we heard people coming in all directions. We were trapped. I slipped into a room with pure white walls. I felt like I was in a void, and Savannah seemed like she was a little scared.

"What's wrong?" I asked. She just froze.

I wanted to talk to her, but something in my gut told me that I shouldn't. I started to break into a cold sweat from the tension.

She looked at me, and her eyes told me that something was coming.

"The council is coming to a crash without the boss! We need to come to an agreement," a lady said, but I couldn't see her. Then a male voice came; it was small and nervous.

"Yes, but we don't have the resources. We are stuck here forever. We should just quit." He sounded like he had been sobbing.

Then, out of nowhere, I saw people coming out of the void. Their bodies formed from what seemed like mist, deeper into the void. Their voices were echoing, and they were coming toward us. "There's nowhere to hide," Savannah said. I scanned the room, and there was nothing but white. We turned around to leave, but the door wasn't there.

"Where's the door?" I asked.

"I don't know."

"Hmmm...maybe if we go farther into the void, they won't be able to see us. Like how we couldn't see them," I suggested. They were getting closer, and their voices were getting louder, so loud that my ears were hurting. As they came closer, we backed into a corner hoping that they couldn't see us. They stopped about thirty feet away from us.

"Well, what do you suppose we do?" asked a new voice.

"I suppose that we should find our gadgets and put them together to blast us out of here."

"Well, that plan is great except for the fact that THAT WILL TAKE YEARS!!!" the man's voice said. Suddenly Savannah gasped and held her breath.

"What's wrong?" I asked. She just held her breath and closed her eyes. I kept listening, and then I turned to her and saw her brown skin turning red at the cheeks. "You can't suffocate yourself," I reminded her. It was like she was in a trance. "What's wrong, Savannah!?" I asked her. "SAVANNAH!" I shook her by her shoulders. I couldn't tell what was wrong with her. Then the people that were talking saw us.

"Hey! Who are you?" a woman asked. Usually Savannah stepped in and made an excuse, but she was just frozen.

"We—I—She—Well, uh...We are here because we are...STUDYING! Y-yes. Studying the, uh, the rooms," I said.

"Studying the rooms?" the woman said.

"Yes."

"What about them?"

"The uh, texture?"

"You don't sound sure."

"Oh, I am! Super texture-y and stuff."

"Texture-y isn't a word."

"Word isn't a word."

"What?"

"Um...Bananas!"

"Bananas?"

"NO! Oranges?"

"What in the world are you talking about?"

The walls, they feel like...bananas and oranges...smoothie?"

"I like banana smoothies."

"Me too...uh, yeah. Feel the walls!"

"Oooh, this is...not like SMOOTHIES!"

By then I was gone. Right before I went deeper into the void, I realized I *forgot* Savannah! I ran back to her, and by the time I got back, the void people were puppy-guarding her. I walked toward them, and they all flinched forward, leaning toward me.

"How can I know you won't hurt me?" I asked.

"You...you are like royalty, you are important to this society. More than the council." I ignored them, thinking they were toying with me.

"If you were to get hurt, we would pay a *large* price for that," the woman said.

"And *not* the money kind," a guy added.

I couldn't tell if they were telling the truth. "I wish this place had a gadget that could break me outta here," I groaned as a gadget popped out of the wall. I picked it up. It had a tag on it that read, 'Chainsaw and laser! O'spylies.'

I popped the top off the gadget, thinking about how Savannah did it. The top was hard to take off. Then I realized it wasn't a top. I had broken the gadget. Gears and liquid were coming out. The liquid dropped on my shoe and almost melted through. I took off my shoe quickly before it touched my toe. I saw a hole in my shoe as the liquid kept dripping out of the gadget.

The laser part definitely *wasn't* going to work out. "I wish this chainsaw thing would come out," I mumbled. Then a miniature chainsaw popped out the top. *"Seriously?"* I sighed and started to cut through the wall. In about an hour, my hands were red from holding the mini chainsaw so long. I cut a full circle, and I had to get something to push it in. "Hey! Can I get something to push this in?" I called to the wall. Nothing happened. "Oh, *now* you don't want to work," I said.

I had to find something to push this open. I tried to push it open with my arms; it *did not* work. I had no idea what to do when a laser beam came and knocked out the circle. "Who—" I looked back and saw Savannah pointing a gadget at the circle. "Savannah! You can move now? I have *so* many QUESTIONS!" I said excitedly.

"Let's...just get...outta here...before...the circle...closes." She sounded *super* exhausted. She was walking slowly like she was in a wedding.

Step, step, stop. Step, step, stop. "Are you okay?" I asked her.

"Of...course," she huffed.

"I don't think so," I mumbled. I helped her to the door, and when we walked out, we were back in the hallway. "You can't tell me *that's* tech," I said, smiling at Savannah.

"It...is...not," she said. I frowned.

"Where were we?" I asked.

One lady stepped up, "Well, we were in a void, Miss."

"Miss?"

"Yes. Oh! Would you like me to call you ma'am?"

"Uh—excuse me?"

Then a man speed-walked in front of me. He was old and a little gray, small and pale with a nervous look on his face. I'll call him Ronald.

"Ms. E is missing, Ma'am. We don't know what to do." By now we were walking down the empty hallways of a building that I'd never seen before. "Ms. *Ellison*?" I thought.

"Ms. E?"

"Yes, the boss. She is somewhere in the building, or at least we think she is."

"Right. So why were you in a void?"

"Well, it was all a blur. But we were thrown in by *someone*."

"Why didn't you escape using your spy

gadgets? You are spies, right?"

"Why, of course."

"So why were you in the void?"

"Well, before we were thrown in, they took all of our gadgets. Except for one, my ankle laser."

"Why didn't you use that?"

"We, um—it got lost in the midst of the void."

"Can...we get...outta...here?" Savannah asked, out of breath. We walked out of the circle but got stuck back in the hallways.

"Wait. How did we end up here?" I asked.

"I think we're trapped," Ronald said.

"Well, yes. But..." We went around five more times, and then I looked out of the window. "Looks like we have another window fall." I looked at Savannah wondering about the way she was acting. I wondered what happened to her.

Savannah's Reality

(Narrated by Savannah)

Harper kept looking at me, but I couldn't stop thinking about what I'd seen in the void.

When I went into that weird state, I saw a purple wall with teal paintings of flowers hanging up. Then I saw a woman with curly brown hair wearing a pink blazer. Then the image went to some lady talking to the council.

"Mrs. Ellison, we were wondering if the funding for gadgets could be expanded for the next mission," one of the council members said.

"Well, how much do you want to raise the fund?" Mrs. Ellison asked.

"Approximately one hundred fifty-five dollars," the same person said.

"Um, well, I can give you one hundred dollars, but we need the majority of our funds to keep this building," Mrs. Ellison said thoughtfully.

Then I saw another scene. It was Harper with Mrs. Ellison. Harper was grabbing the remote off the floor, and Mrs. Ellison was sitting on a sofa. Harper sat down, and the news came on. Then I flashed into a different scene.

Mrs. Ellison was walking in the hallway of a hotel. "Hello, sir," Mrs. Ellison said as Ben walked up. He was in some crazy disguise; I barely recognized him.

"Hello, I appear to be lost. I'm looking for the second elevator. Do you know where it is?" Ben asked.

"Of course, right this way."

Then it showed the inside of the elevator and a big lumpy bag. Mrs. Ellison's voice was calling out of the bag, shouting, "Let me out!"

Then the elevator went to the second floor. Ben pressed the last floor button, and when it got there, he pulled out a gadget. It was flashing blue, yellow, and red over and over.

The elevator started to move again. The meter that told the floor number was blank. Then he placed the gadget on the elevators, and it stopped completely. Nothing happened for a while, then the doors exploded. He walked out with the bag, and it went blank. I was lost in thought for a while, and Harper began to notice. I tried to cover it up by talking, but it didn't come out right. Suddenly, I came back to reality.

"You good?" Harper asked me.

"Wow," I said.

"What?" Harper asked.

"Wow," I repeated.

"Savannah!" she yelled.

"Wow," I said a third time.

"HELLO?" she asked irritatedly.

"Whoa, hey." I noticed I was sweating, and I was kinda sleepy.

"HEY?" Harper yelled. "What do you mean, *'Hey'*? Do you know how worried I was?"

"Yeah," I answered truthfully.

"So why—wait, you could see me?" she asked.

"Yeah," I repeated.

"So why were you all groggy?" she asked, sounding concerned.

"Uh..." I felt like I shouldn't say it in front of the council. So I waited until they went into the far corner of the hall. "I—I saw your mom get *kidnapped*," I told Harper. She laughed in denial.

"I'm serious, Harper, I saw your mom!" She teared up and was pretty angry. I tried to calm her down, but she wouldn't. Now I really didn't have the guts to tell her about seeing her mom as the *company boss*.

I tried to hug her, but she didn't hug me back. "I—I—I can prove it," I said. I wasn't huffing anymore.

She looked up. "How?" she said with quite the attitude. "It's not like tech can fix this, and there's *'no such thing as magic,'"* she said with air quotes.

"I'm *sorry*, Harper. That you lost your mom. I've lost too, though. My dad, my sister, and it's not like Ma—Mother—cares about me. And I'm a freakin' spy!"

I sat on the floor and planted my chin in my palm.

Harper crossed her arms. "There you go! Why do you want to *steal* all the attention? Why do you even care?" Harper threw up her hands.

"I'm *not* taking *any* ATTENTION! I care because I—you—you're my best and *only* friend! Sorry I'm sensitive for you—about you! I *care* Harper, I care!" I told her. Calling her my friend sounded a little good.

"Quit it, Savannah!" Harper turned around, looking mad.

"I want you to *listen* to me," I tried reasoning with her. She tried to open the window. "Harper, please! I—"

"I DON'T CARE, SAVANNAH!" she yelled.

I looked down. "HARPER! I can prove it. *Please.*"

Harper sighed. "*Fine.* Prove your *stupid* little game. But in the meantime..."

She turned to the council, who seemed to be trying to eavesdrop. "I assume that you guys were spies." She looked hopefully at them.

"They weren't exactly spies," I said.

"And how would you know?" she asked.

I didn't answer her because the council was listening in. Though they seemed okay.

"May I?" the woman said.

"Uh, sure?" said Harper.

The woman stepped up, and her black ponytail waved behind her. "We were the head council. We discussed matters with Ms. E."

"Okay...So you aren't spies?" I asked.

"No," the woman said.

"This will be hard." Harper looked out of the window with her back still toward me. "Can you guys jump out of a window?" she asked.

"We surely can," a guy with blonde hair said.

"Okay," I said.

Harper took off her jacket and was trying to open the window again. "It's a little stuck." She exhaled. Then she started trying to open it at a different angle.

Out of the corner of my eye, I saw someone. She was blonde, had a black streak of hair, and wore a sleeveless jean top and biker shorts. She was holding a stun gun.

"Willow," I said under my breath, talking mostly to myself. "Harper," I tapped Harper on her shoulder, "it's Willow. Look."

She still looked mad and said, "Oh man. Willow!"

"She's got a stun gun! We gotta split!"

We tried to open the window, but it didn't budge.

"*You*," Willow said angrily.

Willow was right by us. She pulled out the same little black gadget as before and tried to place it in front of the council. I hit it out of her hand before she could, and she picked it up quickly. Then she placed it over the window.

The same pool of purple, gooey stuff opened up. It flooded over us, and I felt kind of tingly. When it went over my hair, I got pretty mad because I had just washed it. The goo flooded to the council all the way on the other side of the hall. Then the goo drained back into the black thing.

"DNA transferred," a robotic voice said. Harper slapped the gadget off of the wall and crushed it with her shoe. She pushed Willow backward, and I examined myself. I looked the same, and the tingle was just leaving.

All I knew was that she was against us. The gadget must've melted a small hole in the window, because I saw an open spot. I broke the window from the melted spot. Willow started scanning the walls as if she didn't notice us. We climbed out and jumped.

"They got away!" Willow spoke. She must've had an earpiece. Harper helped the council out.

"Now. Prove it, Savannah," Harper said once everyone was on the ground.

I pulled a small gadget from my pocket. I always kept a gadget for every situation, and luckily this one came in handy. It was shiny and white with small specks of red.

"Hold this, pointing to my head. Then go into files. After that, enter memory files;

it's probably in left-brain files. Be careful, I don't want brain damage." Harper held it up, clicked a few times and put a hand over her mouth, surprised.

First, she said, "My mom owns a pink blazer?" She smiled, then frowned. "I—I don't know what to say." She kept replaying the video, and it was giving me a bad headache.

"Can you stop that, please? It hurts."

She backed away and exhaled as if trying to toughen up. "I'm sorry I didn't believe you."

"I accep—" In a split second, Willow slammed on top of her, and they were on the floor. For a second they both looked puzzled, and then I saw an angry flash in Willow's eyes when she looked at me. Then Willow stunned me asleep.

"You wonnnn't get awayyyy thaat fassst!" I said. Harper pushed Willow, then Willow fell over, and her hand hit me. "Hey, I'm not in this fight!" I said, confused.

"You are now," Willow hissed.

Then everything paused. Willow stopped running over to Harper. Harper stopped running, and I stopped squirming.

"What—" I said.

Willow gulped and slowly stood up from her running position. Her eyes were bulging, and then a helicopter the size of three elephants came towering over us. When it landed, it nearly cut five trees in its path. A man that was, like, six feet tall came out; he looked like he'd had a fight with a tree and lost the fight—HARD.

He had a scratch over his left cheek and a scar across his forehead. He overlooked Harper and me but stuck his eyes on Willow.

"I've given you multiple extensions," he spoke in a raspy, scratchy voice.

"Someone get this man a lozenge," I mumbled as I slowly stood, regaining my balance. He didn't even glare at me. He was skinny and wore a dark tux.

"Yes, sir." Willow sounded like she was about to cry.

"So now that you've basically failed, finish these kids off."

Back to Harper

Today was already going worse than bad. Now we had to fight Willow. She turned her back to the man and looked at us. She sighed as if she didn't want to, but she lunged at me. I tried to grab her by the shoulders and swing her around, but she was *angry*, and she fought harder than I thought she ever could. Right when I was about to grab her shoulders, she dropped down, grabbed my leg, and tripped me. I was on the floor now, weeping from the pain in my back. She leaped over me and ran for Savannah. From what I could see,

Savannah dodged Willow's first punch and went in for a kick.

But Willow slid under Savannah's kick and pushed her from the behind.

Savannah turned around and went for another kick; this time, she got her right in the gut.

But Willow acted as if Savannah's kick was as soft as a pillow because she jammed her palm into Savannah's face, and Savannah fell backwards.

Willow turned to me, who was in a crawling pose, and she pulled my arm and swung me around so many times I got dizzy and hit something hard. I didn't pass out completely, but I was confused.

She ran to the side of the building and went for the people we'd found in the void. They all scrambled into one little bunch, and then she just looked at them. She turned to the scar-faced man who then nodded to her, and she pulled something out of her pocket.

It was a nice shade of purple, and it was flaming blue. She threw it at the people, and it formed a bag around them; she picked it up and threw it in the helicopter.

"Finish your mission." And with that, the man was gone. I couldn't move my head, but I saw Savannah's leg. *"I hope she's okay..."* I drifted off. I was moving, no, rolling somewhere. I hadn't opened my eyes, but I could tell that I was moving. When I opened my eyes, I saw Savannah lying on the floor, and I was rolling OFF THE BED! I was too late, though. *SPLAT*—and my face was flat on the floor. *"Owwww."* I struggled to get up, but I found out that I was in my dorm room with Savannah. "Savannah?" I said. She opened her eyes and managed a smile. "What happened out there?" I asked.

"Well..." She started to get up. "We were apologizing, and then, out of nowhere, Willow came flying down the roof onto you; then we started fighting, then a big helicopter came flying in and a tall man came and told Willow that she'd had many extensions and that she needed to finish us off; then we fought and she started tripping you; then she came to me and pushed me in the face, then it went dark, then I woke up for a sec and saw her throw you into a tree, then it went black again, and I woke up in here." She didn't breathe while she was saying that, so now she was inhaling a bunch of air.

"WHOO!" Savannah huffed.

"So I hit a tree?" I asked.

"Yep," she said.

"How'd we end up here?" I asked.

"No idea."

I walked over to the door and tried to open it, but it wouldn't budge. "The door is locked," I said. She got up, paced the room, and started mumbling things to herself.

"Where's the council? How do we get outta here? Are the walls caving in? Why is it all of a sudden so hard to breathe?" she asked herself, breathing deeply.

"I think you—" I started.

"I'm losing it," she told herself. "Right, Harper? I'm losing it, aren't I?" she asked.

"Well—" I started.

"Yep," she confirmed.

"You aren't listening to me." I frowned.

"I am listening. I am sooo listening that my ears are—are so big right now I can hear your heartbeat!" She started jumping up and down.

"*HUH?*" I wondered.

"Ha! Ha. Ha. Ha. Ha! This is all okay! I'm—I'm ALL GOOD HERE!! Ha, ha!" She smiled and started breathing deeply again.

"I'm starting to think you are losing it," I told her.

"No, I'm having a—"

Suddenly, she stopped and crumpled to the ground as if she were having a sugar crush after that sugar *rush*. I didn't know what was wrong with her. But I thought she had anxiety. While she was on the floor, I focused on getting us out. There was no trace of Willow, and I couldn't find anything to prove she was evil. I thought about breaking down the doors, but I didn't want to draw too much attention to myself. Savannah was still out for a second. I wondered how she always had a gadget on her.

She'd said, *"There's no magic here, just skill."*

"Maybe if I use my skill...PRANKS!" I emptied all of my and Savannah's pockets. She had what looked like a squirt gun, a small safety-pin-shaped thing, an M&M, and a multicolored pen. I had a piece of lint, a shiny penny, a Monopoly Chance card, and a noisemaker I took from Simon (the sounds were so annoying). I knew the things Savannah had couldn't be what they seemed to be—I mean, she's a spy! I took out the squirt gun, aimed it at the beds, and pulled the plastic trigger.

I saw it squirt out water, but the water

turned the bed into a marble. The marble rolled to me, and the gun had a small voice that said, "Contained." It sounded like a robot. I picked up the marble and saw that the bed had shrunken inside it.

"Ok," I mumbled, "containment squirty." I took out the safety pin. "How do I test this?" I wondered. I clipped the pin to my jacket, and it began to form a hole in the material. I ripped it off of my jacket and clipped it to the carpet.

I realized this gadget must be for escaping bags. That made me think of my mom. "Open-this-bag pin," I named the gadget. I thought about the M&M. It was too risky to try and eat it, so I decided to simulate eating it instead. I went to the bathroom and turned on the sink for "saliva," then I put it on the floor and smashed it with my foot for the "chewing." It started to enlarge, getting bigger and bigger.

Then it almost popped—until I took it out and dried it with my shirt corner. "And I'll save you; I can use that...how about Mr. M&M?" I took up the multicolored pen and clicked the purple tip. A huge purple foam obscured the room, making it hard to see. I clicked the purple again, and the foam sucked in. "Okay! I'll call you Foam." I cracked the marble in front of the door and climbed atop the bed. I put the squirt gun over the door so that when someone opened the door it would squirt over them.

Then I turned back to the carpet, where I'd clipped the pin. A hole had formed there, and I planned to have the marble roll into it. I dropped the M&M in the hole and tested the blue tip on the pen. Just as I thought, it sprayed water. I waited for someone to walk in, aiming the pen at the hole and ready to click the blue tip. I knew this wouldn't backfire.

I waited for the door to open for about two hours. No one entered. I started to wonder why I thought someone would actually come in. My arm was getting tired, so I put it down for a second. Then I saw the doorknob slowly turning, and I pulled my hand back up. Willow started to walk in. I snatched up the gun and pulled the trigger. She was absorbed into the marble and rolled, then she fell into the hole. I sprayed the M&M, which started to blow up in size. After that, I saw the spray was growing so big that the marble went flying through the room. Then the prank backfired. The marble hit the roof and cracked.

Willow came out, but fell down, unprepared. I pressed the first color tip I could— it was red, and party lasers shot out of the pen. I switched to yellow, and a box popped out with a "Sharing Size" bag of M&Ms

inside. This I could use. I poured it out onto the floor in front of Willow, then I started to stomp and shoot with the blue tip. The M&Ms enlarged and pushed Willow to the far wall.

There was a long pause before I finally took a breath. That all happened so fast. I peeked around Savannah, who was still on the floor, and saw Willow. Her face was smashed from the M&M blowout. I pulled her out of it, making sure she didn't suffocate. I was probably already getting expelled from this school, I thought; I couldn't be a murderer too. I finally got a good look at her.

She looked bad. Her face was really pale, and her eye was twitching. I thought about going over and poking her, but I had seen the movies, and poking *never* went well. Instead I waved my hand in front of her. She blinked and reset herself. "Look...I am too tired to fight. But I'm not giving up," I said.

She looked relieved for a minute, but then

a sad expression was on her face. "I know," she said, like it hurt to say.

"What does *that* mean?" I asked.

"I know you're tired and you won't give up," she told me.

"Are you *surrendering?*"

"No," she said firmly.

"Is this a joke? 'Cause if it's a joke, then, uh...I'm armed with really special...gadgets," I threatened awkwardly.

"It's not a joke," she said, her face a stone. "But I need your help."

I started laughing so hard my stomach started to hurt. "Thi—this is hilarious!!!" I said between laughs.

"I know, and I'm sorry for what happened back outside."

By this point I was cracking up, not knowing she was serious. "Ahhhh, Willow, didn't know you'd be good for a laugh." I cautiously patted her on the shoulder. Her face lay emotionless, and her eyes were becoming white again. "Ohhh, you're *not* kidding?" She shook her head, looking down at Savannah.

"Did I do that?" Willow asked.

"No," I told her.

"Then what happened?" she asked.

"She, uhh, well...I *think* she had an anxiety attack or something." I said, not sure.

"Ohhhh. So are you going to help me or not?" she asked.

"Ok. Lemme get this straight. You tried multiple times to kill us, and now you want us to *help* you?" I said sarcastically.

"Yes. And I'm not apologizing again so work with what you've got," Willow said, not joking.

"Do I need to repeat myself—y'know, the whole 'get this straight' thing? Because that sounded pretty crazy," I said.

"No, you don't need to repeat yourself," Willow said.

"Ok, say sorry. Or else," I demanded,

almost like Mr. Kaleb.

"Or else what?" she asked. I felt her guard rising up.

"Or you don't want my help *that* bad." I said.

"I...am...fine, sorry. There, happy?" she sneered.

"Very," I smiled.

"Ok," she murmured.

"Now what is it you *need* my help with?" I asked, emphasizing the fact that she "needed" my help.

"The scar-face guy is, uh, well, he told me I totally failed, and he needs me to make you come with me—the rest is classified. I told him you guys are total dorks and we definitely don't need you. I also told him about the roof, and he was like, 'And you throwing her off the roof was a save—'"

"Oh, get to the point, huh?"

"HE'S AFTER YOUR MOM!" she said loudly.

"How'd he—ah, I know what this is! You are trying to get me to confess! Not gonna work," I said, very spy-like.

Willow showed me the video I saw in Savannah's brain files. "I've seen enough!" I said as I pushed the screen she held out of my face.

"*You*," Savannah pointed at Willow shakily. "You are Tree? No, Vine?"

"Willow," I said.

"WILLOW! You fought me! You threw me off the roof!" Apparently, Savannah was still drowsy. "You wanna fight me, then? Come on, girlfriend, 'cause we are about to go into it!" She held up her fists.

"Hey, hey." Willow walked to her, about to push her fists down.

WHAM! Savannah hit her and put an M&M right on her chin, then grabbed the squirt gun (she was just a bit taller than me, so she could reach) and said, "Enjoy your marble, TREE."

She almost marbled her when I purple-foamed the room, and instead of Willow, the foam got contained. I pulled the foam that was now in a marble back into the pen.

"SAVANNAH, please. Listen to reason." I helped her to the bed, and Willow stood uncomfortably in the mirror examining the pink spot that Savannah had created on her head. I thought for a moment and considered what I was saying.

"Do you have anxiety?" I asked.

"What?" She looked down at her hands.

"Do you?" I asked again.

"Why does it matter? I mean, I'm fine," she said.

"Fine is clearly not good enough, considering what happened before you passed out," I told her.

"Fine IS and WILL ALWAYS be good enough for me." She had a determined look.

"How can you explain the business before you passed out?" I asked.

"Well, I—of course, I hit my head on the tree too hard. *Duh!*" She extended her neck in proof.

"That makes sense, but what about you muttering?" I asked.

"What muttering?" She asked.

"At night. When I came back from the fence, you were muttering to yourself."

"So?" she said.

"And you were muttering to yourself earlier," I told her.

"What's the problem if I mutter a little? No biggie," she said.

"I think it's a pretty big biggie." I said.

"Why? No one is getting hurt."

"Well...I guess you should at least try to get rid of it," I said.

"How do I do that? I mean, I am a spy. I don't have time for some boring anxiety vaccines," she told me.

"First off, there isn't an anxiety vaccine. Second, when is your next mission?"

"Uhhh..." She looked at the calendar that hung right over her bed. "Next week. Nebraska," she said.

"Good. In Nebraska, you could get a therapist," I told her.

"How, if I'm moving from state to state every month?" she asked.

"You could just have that one for the period of time that you're there," I told her.

She sighed and rested her head on the bed frame.

Then memories of the mind clip I saw came up: a rush of anger, sadness, and confusion ran through my body. I looked to the door where Willow stood, still rubbing her head where a bump was forming.

"Let's go," I said. Willow brushed her hair back. I looked back to Savannah. "You gonna be okay here alone?" I asked.

"Yes." She slid under the covers. We closed the doors quickly.

"So, th—they're after my mom?" I asked.

"Yeah. They need to—find her," Willow hesitated.

"How can I help?" I asked.

"You? Help? Eh," she said.

I blinked. "So," I asked, "what should we talk about?"

"WE don't need to talk about anything. This will all be over if you follow my directions, so no talking. Just following directions." She grinned at herself.

I noticed how empty the school was. "How come all of the students are gone?" I asked, peeking into someone else's room.

"I made Kaleb lock them all in...a holding place," she mused.

I stopped dead in my tracks. "Where is the council?" I asked.

She noticed I stopped and turned around. "With the students...now we're doing more talking than following directions," she said and kept on ahead of me.

"What's the plan?" I asked.

Willow balled her fists at her sides and slightly motioned her chin to the cameras in the hallway. I nodded and walked by, probably less normally than I wanted to. Willow took us out to a familiar place: the fence.

It was up now, but it still looked different. Close up it looked plain, gray, dull. It used to have a shine, silver and bright. She looked around as if she were afraid we were being watched.

"What's wrong?" I whispered.

"Nothing. Just following all of the procedures."

"So..."

"The plan, right. I am supposed to destroy you; my boss needs you out of the way."

My eyes bulged. "Well, I'm not just gonna *let* you destroy me."

"That's where I need your help—"

"I'm not going to cooperate with you ya-know-whatting me. I have a life to get back to."

"I know, which is why I need you to come with me, pretend to be dead, and pretend to stay out of the way," she explained.

I thought about this. Nothing seemed too wrong, I thought. "All right, but on one condition. You have to explain more when we're done."

"Explain what?"

"Y'know, like *why are you destroying me?*"

"Ok. But I'm not destroying you, I—it's like WWE. They fake punches and stuff. So you'll fake *being destroyed.*"

"Okay, I don't have practice with that. I can—"

"No. No practice."

"Then how do I get good with faking?" She put her index finger on her chin and squinted her eyes.

The sunset darkened. Her hair blew in her face. I felt a little better as the wind blew past me. Then Willow looked puzzled. She ran to me, grabbed my leg, and flipped me over on my back. The look in her eyes was fear and anger; she pinched me and I screamed, then she touched my temples and my eyes closed. I could hear everything, but I couldn't see.

"Sir...I didn't know you were coming so early, i-is my deadline over? If so, I—"

"Silence!" the voice boomed. "There is a change of plans."

I opened my eyes a little and saw him whispering into her ear. Willow was pressing her hands together so hard her knuckles turned white. "Uh, ok?" She shifted her weight.

"So, I assume that you've at least gotten the first phase of the plan over with?" he mused.

"I'm kinda in session." She pointed toward me and motioned for me to close my eyes.

"Well, then. Sorry for the bother." He checked his watch. "You know what to do. I have matters to attend to. Tyler is on thin ice." Then his voice faded.

I waited about ten minutes to open my eyes, and Willow was looking over at me. "What did you do to me?" I asked, rubbing my throbbing temples.

"I did a *jogo de pressão nas têmporas.*" She picked her nail.

"A what?"

"A temple-pressure play...Portuguese, duh."

"You know Portuguese?"

"When you go from country to country, you pick up some things. Come on, we have to go to my base."

"Your *base?*"

"My base. The place where no one can get to. It's not a long walk."

"Oh. Why? And how long is the walk?"

"You ask a lot of questions."

"I've been told that before."

"It's true. Anyhow, that information is classified. Less questions, more following directions. We'd better start moving faster."

A Clubhouse Base Full of Traps

"Don't step there." Willow pointed to a spot on the floor. I quickly ran over it and looked behind me as a hole opened in the floor.

"Thanks," I said as I stared at Willow, hopping over cracks in the floor as deadly traps appeared.

"What's the problem?" Willow asked.

I hesitated and shrugged. "I don't understand. Are you trying to kill someone?"

"No, I just have to keep this place hidden," she said, jumping over spikes.

"A little help here?" I asked as I stood, not moving.

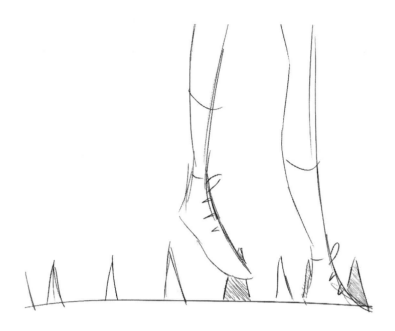

"Here!" she squirted me with a squirt gun, and I became a marble. I stood in the small space, shrunken.

"Hey! How did you get that?!" I called out, but my voice was obscured and nearly silent. I tried to crack the marble, but I realized Willow would crack it. I watched from the thin pockets of Willow's side belt. There were holes, fires, spikes, and arrows. *I wonder how much she comes here,* I thought.

She threw me to the ground, and the

marble cracked. I landed on my hands in a handstand. I flipped over and saw Willow fanning herself as her hair stuck to her sweaty forehead.

"Those fires were that hot?" I asked.

"What? Oh, yeah," she said.

"So, what's this breaking stuff? You know that you told me that's what you were scared of," she said, not looking me in the eye. I barely knew what it was myself.

"Mmm. What smells so good?" I asked, changing the subject.

"Nothing is cooking." She smelled the air. "I'm gonna make po'boys; you want some?" Willow asked, taking out bread.

"Um. Sure, I haven't eaten for a while, now that I think about it."

Willow pulled frozen shrimp from her freezer. She put the shrimp on a metal scrap and turned on her little burner.

"Hey, we use those to cook when we go camping!" I pointed at her burner.

"And I call it luxury." She rolled her eyes. "Do you want anything on yours?"

"I don't know, put the usual," I said as she took out a small piece of lettuce and a cherry tomato. "You don't have many supplies here, do you?"

"You," she said. "Talking break." She pointed to an old, stained sofa. Something about her is so demanding I have to listen.

"Okay, jeez," I said.

"Hmph," she said, pointing to the sofa again.

I examined the bunker. It was messy but comforting...in a way. The walls were different colors: one wall was bright yellow, the other was dark purple, another blue and green and orange, all colors. She had two rooms from what I could see. It was awfully hot, and there were no windows. Dust covered a fan in the corner of the room. To me it didn't look too functional in its condition.

A little-kid's-sized shorts and shirt lay across the floor halfway under the couch, as if she had lived here for a long time. Willow was sitting at a small table that was shabby and had a bad paint job.

"So this is where you live," I said. She glared at me. "Well, technically, it wasn't a question," I reminded her. She took the last bite of her po'boy and wiped her greasy hands on a napkin that seemed used. "I see you skipped spring cleaning?" I asked as she placed my po'boy in front of me.

"Well, little miss 'everyone has to be just like me, a neat freak,' I don't come here so often to clean."

She picked up her plate and dropped it into the trash can with a bunch of sass.

"Well, *excuse* me!" I said, trying to equally challenge her sass with shrimp in my mouth.

"Come on. This is your room." I finished the po'boy as she led me through a short hallway with portraits of faces. I stopped in front of one that reminded me of me. It had a white background and different colors splattered everywhere.

"Do you paint all of these?" I asked, pointing to the painting. She ran up to me and grabbed my wrist.

"Don't touch the paintings." After that she practically dragged me by the arm through her bunker. Finally we reached a room that smelled like mildew and leftover gym socks. It looked like a place built out of a junkyard. The bed springs poked out on the sides, the pillows had holes in them, and the walls had dents.

"What happened here?" I said, pinching my nose.

"I, uh...went through a phase," she said.

"Right. A very *serious* phase," I told her.

"It was serious, okay, but this is how you're going to have to deal with it. This is where you will rest until we leave later on today," she said, sadly.

I could've sworn that I saw tears in her eyes when she turned away and went into her room, which was right across from mine. I picked up a pillow and shook it out. Dust came flying out until basically the whole pillow stuffing was gone. "Does she fill her pillows with dust?" I muttered to myself, checking the other pillows. There was a blanket tossed on the floor and a jacket sitting on a small chair. I looked over the bed, disgusted.

"Is there a bathroom here?" I asked.

"Sure," she said, "but, it doesn't have proper plumbing."

I grimaced. "Too late." I looked at the sink pipes through the open bathroom door. They were dripping a *lot*. "Do you have, um, a washing machine?" I asked.

"Ugh," she answered, annoyed.

I walked into her room. "Um, in English?" She was reading a book titled *The Wizard's Heir*. She was about halfway through it.

"You must not have heard me: WASHING MACHINE," I said.

"Stop. I don't care. If you want luxury- I don't know, go to the luxury hotel! I don't really care," she mumbled, shooing me away.

"I might just do so, MS. ATTITUDE!" I said, pointing at her.

"I *don't* have *any* sort of *attitude, I* have- a brain and emotions," she said matter-of-factly.

I didn't know if I should use my famous mid-argument brother attack or my well-known croc tears when losing an argument. I decided that croc tears were good, but then I stopped, realizing that she had been through a lot. I kinda sympathized with how she felt. I'd been through a lot, too. I remembered Dad. *Did he know about Mom being a spy lady? Had he been lying to us? Was Mom lying?* It all flew into my brain in a bunch, filling me up with mixed emotions. A rush of anger and sadness spread to my fingertips, and it burned.

"Ohhhh! She's feelin' it!" Willow jumped out of her bed and threw the book at the wall. (That's probably where the dents in my bedroom wall came from.) She had a huge smile on her face. My mouth wouldn't speak. I wanted to ask her what was happening, but everything froze.

"Am I in shock?" I managed. I sounded like I hadn't drunk water in months. Willow was inching forward and grabbed me by the arm.

"You're not in shock. You're getting into it," she told me.

"Getting into what?" I almost yelled.

"The zone. Finally!" She sat me in a chair and ran around in a circle. I sat in the chair as my fingers were burning and my emotions were sparking like fireworks.

"What is happening?!" I felt like I was in the middle of an earthquake.

"I already told you. Now don't talk. It will mess up the process." She sat across from me and put her chin in her hands, smiling like she just won a million dollars. She watched me for hours until the burning sensation stopped. She got up, disappointed, and sat on the other chair to the side of me. She studied me for a few minutes before I came back to normal.

"Well...you wanna explain what happened?" I asked.

"Well," she sighed, "you got the SOS. Stage of the Spies," she said.

"Is that some type of cooties?"

"No...just a thing that spies get; it's basically, uh, a spark. When your spark activates, your spy instinct kicks in," she told me.

"All I want to know is...IS THIS MAGIC?!" This topic was driving me insane because while Savannah told me that it was all just skill, nothing here seemed like skill. Nothing was making sense.

"Well...no," she sighed and rubbed her eyes. "It's just emotions, mostly, loss..." She drifted off and shot back up again. "Anyway, why didn't you do it fully?" she asked.

"What do you mean?" I asked.

"Like, you're not supposed to be done yet." She said, looking me up and down.

"Done what?" I wondered out loud.

"Y'know...formulating! The process, it's not supposed to end like this." She ran over to her room and got an iPad, which was on a charger that hung out of the wall a little.

"Uh, so I'm formulating?" I looked over to her with her back hunched over the iPad, her eyes glued to the screen. When I stood up, my legs felt tingly, but I still had all of my body parts, as far as I could see. I walked over to her and peeked at her screen. She had a picture of the spy agency, pictures of me, pictures of Savannah, and more.

"Hey!" She shot up as fast as a bullet and jumped in the air.

"There it is! It makes sense." She pushed me onto the couch and lifted my chin. "So how did you feel when you were having your spark?" she asked.

"I mean, I was feeling mixed emotions and like a bur—" I started.

"—ning sensation! You're on stage..." She scrolled on her iPad. "One! You'll be going through multiple stages. It seems as if your spy zing is taking its sweet, sweet, time," she sighed.

I studied her face as she obsessed over my "spark." She looked so happy.

"So, you like these sparks?" I asked.

"Yeah, they are all I've wanted to know about," she said.

"Didn't you have yours already? I mean, you are a pretty good spy," I told her.

"I'm not a spy," she answered quickly.

"Well, then what are you? How did you..."

"I am a student. At school," she responded even more quickly.

"So you work for that guy. What is your mission?" I asked.

"It's not a mission. Speaking of that guy, we have to get moving. I have to meet him," she said.

"Meet him where?" I said.

"At a place." She paused. "I'm not against you; I actually want to be on your side. But I can't flunk this mission. It could define my whole future. So I'm just going to tell you: my mission is to take you to him. When I take you to him, then he'll get a DNA sample and use that to test the biological weapons that he made based on your mom's files that had her allergies and stuff, and so if his plan works, he'll use those weapons to defeat your mom and take over the spy industries. He didn't tell me the rest, so all I know is that I have to do my part. Also, he's my dad."

We started walking out of the bunker. I was shocked, scared, and most of all confused. When I was back at home with my mom, she would never hide anything—well, I guess I was wrong.

How could the scar-faced man be Willow's dad? I mean, he was all scary and mean, but now that I think of it, they both had that demanding tone in their voices. That skin that was pale most of the time. I thought about how she had her black streak of hair, then I thought about how the scar-faced guy had that scar. Willow would look good with a scar on her face.

"Why didn't he just get my mom?" I considered what I was saying. I didn't really want my mom to be captured; I hoped I didn't give Willow and her scary dad any ideas. He could be listening in on our conversations right now!

"He did have her," she said.

"Did? Where is she?" I asked.

"We don't know," she answered.

"When did he get her?" I asked some more.

"He took her from Mexico a few weeks ago—" she started.

"It's been WEEKS?!" I interrupted. I didn't

even consider how long I'd been away from my family.

"Yeah, I mean, I don't know how long *you've* been at that academy. But the scar-faced man took her from a vacation resort a few weeks ago," Willow said.

"So, what I'm hearing is, my mom is like a trading piece for your 'agents'?" I asked, confused.

"Look, I wasn't the one in charge. The only reason I am in this is because your mom escaped. You're the only link to her. You're her only child," she said. *Only child?* She had the wrong information, but I didn't want to tell her that. Although I *did* think that trading with Simon to take my place in this mess would be an accomplishment.

"Uh, right, so we are going to meet him where?" I asked.

"In LA. The place of my dreams, but it *had* to be Culver City," she told me. She reached in her pocket, pulled out a remote, and clicked a button. Nothing happened, but I decided not to ask.

My legs were burning—which was weird since we'd only been walking for fifteen minutes—and I had sweat stains on my shirt. I couldn't even see the bunker from where we were.

"Where *are* we? I know we didn't walk to Culver City."

"We are actually very close to Culver City." She shook the remote in my face. "This little buddy of mine sped us up without us even noticing." Show-off. We walked for a little bit into a small town, and it started getting cold. I looked around. We stood in a huge, empty parking lot behind a building that blocked the sun completely, so it was shaded and breezy. "The driver is supposed to be here. Ugh, she's late." She checked her watch and rolled her eyes. A black Durango slowly pulled into the parking lot.

A Memory and a Scarred Face

Willow tried to open the door, but the driver locked them. "Open the doors!" Willow shouted through the closed window.

I couldn't see the driver or hear her over the breeze that was turning into a strong wind, blowing in my ears, making goosebumps appear on my arms. The driver rolled down the windows and said something to Willow that clearly offended her, because she kicked the side of the car and the driver slammed her hand on the windowsill.

"How dare you speak to me in that tone?

Do you know who I work for?!" Willow started to bang her fist on the side mirror.

I stood there for half an hour until I saw Willow hop through the window, and after that I heard hands slapping and the driver's car door open. The driver ran out and didn't even take a glimpse at me. Willow stepped out slowly and took a deep breath.

"Come on," she said.

I hopped in the car for warmth and waited for another driver to show up, but Willow sat in the driver's seat. "Hey!" I said. She looked at me like there wasn't a huge problem.

"What?" Willow asked innocently.

"What do you think *you're* doing?" I sounded like Mom!

"I'm about to get us to Culver City, obviously."

"Well...when is the driver going to get here?" I asked.

"I'm right here. Are you okay?" she said.

"I'm NOT okay. Okay? Matter of fact, I'm

less than not okay. I hesitate to get in the car with my *grandma!* You think I'm gonna let *you*—a, like, fourteen-year-old—drive me to LA? *Without* a driver's license?" I asked.

"Well, we have to meet him by noon, so yeah." She reached for the start button and pushed it. The sound of the car starting was like a roar in my ears. I flinched and jumped to the backseat.

"Don't drive yet." I said pulling on my seatbelt and the middle seatbelt.

"How rude," she scoffed. She put the car in reverse and pulled out.

I was holding my breath as she did. My hands were squeezing the seats so hard, I was sure my knuckles were white. I could hear my heart beating and my breath going in and out of my lungs. Willow was driving smoothly and calmly with a plain face.

"So…" I slowly ungripped my hands from the seats, "why are you so scared of your dad?" I asked.

She chuckled. "Uh, I never really thought about that. W-why do you think I'm *scared*?" She turned a corner a little too fast for my comfort.

"I just was wondering, because whenever

your dad comes you get really pale and you—
y'know, tighten up."

She sighed and rubbed her head. "Do you need to know everything?" I shifted uncomfortably in my seat. I think she noticed. "I feel you, I mean, you were taken from your home and thrown into a situation you didn't know about. Now all you want are answers. Answers to why things are the way they are. Answers to how things ended up so mixed up. Answers to why your father would change so much after—" She hit the brakes and sighed.

She was describing everything I was feeling—except for the last bit about my father changing. Although I don't think she was talking only about me.

The rest of the ride was silent. My mind was even blank. We pulled into a small parking lot in front of Helms Bakery a few minutes later, around 11:45. The scar-faced man was sitting outside in a sweater and jeans.

He didn't look scary right now. His scar was covered with makeup, which was super weird. I never thought of him as a makeup type of man, though it looked like he knew what he was doing when he put on that makeup. I barely noticed. He was grinning at the waitress, but when he saw us, his expression changed; it turned into a straight, plain face, and he knitted his eyebrows.

The waitress left with an empty tray. Suddenly I was freezing cold. Willow was about to open the door. "Wait. Do the temple thingy."

"I can't. The whole plan is to make sure that he doesn't *actually* get your DNA. So I need you to be completely conscious." She was whispering like he could hear us. She opened her car door, and I opened mine. She ran over to me and put a hand over my shoulder, whispering short sentences without moving her lips.

"Just play along. Follow my lead. Roll with the punches."

I exhaled, and my breath came out white and misty. I examined the ground around us. This was California—no snow, no ice, just plain blacktop. Why was it so freezing? When we walked up to him, his expression softened; he actually had a peachy color on his face now that I really looked at him. Willow's face was fixed and plain. She had her lips pressed together, and she squeezed my shoulder harder as we got closer to him.

The circulation in my arm was being cut off. I tried to shake her off, but her grip was *really* good. There were people around us at their own tables, so that made me feel better. At least the father-daughter combo wouldn't make a scene in front of all these people. One lady looked at us and looked twice at Willow. Willow looked down and sighed, but in the same second, she looked back up with the same face. At this point we were one foot away from her dad.

I guess we were walking very slowly because a car honked at us for walking in their parking spot. We sat at a small table on the right side. I was about to sneeze, but Willow stopped me. She put her hand to her mouth in a fist and looked at me from the side of her eye. "Ahem?" I looked out the window and saw a bird that flew above us started flying in the shape of a D. Then I saw the waitress holding a plate of rolls shaped like an N.

I noticed a mural on the wall with a person who was baking and wore a chef hat with the letter A embroidered on the side. *Now you can't tell me that's not magic*, I thought. Willow was telling me a simple sneeze could have a lot of DNA in it. I straightened my T-shirt collar like a tie. I meant business— once I knew *what* business we were doing.

"Hey, y'all! You want a little somethin'?" the waitress asked. I looked at the rolls shaped in an N on her tray, and I considered grabbing one, but Willow elbowed me in the side really hard.

"Saliva," she muttered under her breath.

"What was that, honey?"

"I'll take two of those rolls and a hot cocoa."

My stomach grumbled, but I knew that everything I loved was at stake, so I shifted in my seat and spoke carefully, making sure my spit didn't spray out at any point. "I won't be eating anything. I'm, uh, allergic to dairy," I lied. The rolls were calling my name. I reached for my water cup and took a sip.

I set my cup down, and the waitress flinched and said, "Here, I—I'll take that. Don't want you eating any bugs."

She reached for my water, but Willow went to grab a napkin; on her way she knocked over my cup of water, and it shattered. She took a glance at her father and got up. She pinched me on her way out.

"Yeesh!" I said under my breath. So much for being careful. Her father motioned her to come behind the building. I could tell the pinch Willow gave me was a sign to stay put, but I couldn't. I casually followed them, acting like I was just taking a stroll. "Willow! What are you doing?" the scar-faced man said.

"I'm sorry, I don't know what's wrong with me," Willow lied.

"Well, then, just let me handle this," he said.

"No," Willow said firmly.

"Huh?" He widened his eyes.

"No. Let me handle this. Get Briana out of here; did you see how she flinched? Harper is going to get suspicious. Let me get the DNA," Willow told him.

Briana? I thought.

"Why should I?" he asked.

"Because you aren't being careful. By the way, she is onto you. What's with the DNA all over the place?" she asked.

"Fine. Meet me in the boiler house. And don't cause a scene. You know what happened last time," Willow's father said.

"Then why did you pick this spot if you knew that I am not exactly the best customer?" Willow asked.

I waited for her dad to answer, but he didn't. I ran back to the table. Willow walked up two seconds after I sat down. Her dad sat down and nodded.

"Come on, Harper." She grabbed my hand and started her squeezing game. My fingers went numb so fast I had to flex them after we reached the bathroom. She opened the door and peeked in. It smelled like what my mom would call *"suciedad."* Thinking about my mom made me more determined to finish this.

Willow started talking to me, but I wasn't listening. I was breathing deep and balling and unballing my fists. My eyes started tearing up, and I think I screamed.

Shades of gold and pictures of my family were swarming around me. I was brought back to memories of my dad throwing me up and down in his arms and my brother and me playing tag when we were smaller. I saw Savannah, lying in the bed once we left her. And I saw Willow slamming into me at the spy academy. I felt like I was falling ten miles a minute off of a cliff.

My stomach was swishing and swooshing every which way until I landed on the floor. It was black. I opened my eyes and I was on the bathroom floor, lying there, practically shaking myself into an earthquake. Willow was staring over me with a worried look on her face. I tried to sit up, but it felt like my spine was being twisted when I tried to move.

"Ahhhhh! What—what was that? What did you do to me?!"

"I didn't *do* anything." I looked at her face and saw she was a little scared.

"Did I scare you?"

She sighed and reluctantly nodded.

This was strange. I was still lying on the bathroom floor, and Willow was scared of me. I rolled over on my stomach and pushed myself up onto my feet with all of my energy.

"You're crossing over, y'know," Willow said flatly.

"Crossing over?" I asked.

"Yeah, you're going into phase two," she said.

"Wow," I said.

"So that's what that was," I said.

"Yeah. But I have to meet him in five minutes." Her phone rang with a little girl singing a song. It went like, "I love livin' in a house with my faaamilyyyy, and I love my brother 'cause we're faaamilyyyy!" She immediately reached into a hidden pocket in her jacket and answered the phone.

"Hi. Okay. No. She is resistant. This is all your fault. *Sor*-ry. Okay. Nope. I don't think so. Bye," Willow said into her phone.

She put her phone back in the hidden pocket and told me to follow close behind her. We walked through the bakery, which smelled of cinnamon and delicious food. We passed the men's bathroom and the counter. We walked out to our table, and Willow reached into another hidden pocket. She grabbed sanitizing wipes and wiped down our table.

The lady who glared at us stared at Willow, and Willow glared back with the same evil eye as her father. The lady looked down until we were out of her sight. We went through an alleyway, down some sidewalks, over a few flights of stairs, and through a few parking lots. Then we stopped at a small building about the size of Grams's casita, but with a padlock about the size of my phone. It was right by the bakery, so I didn't understand why we took the long way.

"How come the building is right there

and we walked for so long?" I asked.

"Because I need to stay away from street cameras." She put in a code on the padlock to the left of the door. There was a banging noise and the sound of metal scraping inside before the door opened. Seven guys all in gray were standing in a triangle around the scar-faced man, who was at the tip of the triangle, looking down at us.

He was in an all-black suit and black dress shoes. His face was pale again in the cold darkness of the room, and he'd taken off his makeup, so his scar showed. He wore a top hat that held a feather in the corner.

"Willow. Harper." He nodded. "I am glad you could make it." One of the guys came up to us and reached for Willow's hand. She held it out, and he examined her palm ever so carefully. He acted like her hand was a delicate jewel. Then he looked at scar-faced man. He lifted his chin to Willow, and she backed away.

"You cannot" she said. The man looked like he understood.

"Cannot what?" I asked.

"Cannot pat me down," she replied, taking off her jacket. "Any of you. Do not touch me unless I allow you." she said like she owned them.

She handed the man her jacket, and she emptied her pockets. He took her jacket and reached into all of the hidden pockets before backing up exactly into the spot he started in. Another guy walked up to me, and Willow held her hand up to him.

"He is making sure that you don't bring any weapons with you to fight them." I nodded.

"Take off your jacket and empty your pockets," he said.

I did. I guess I was all clear, because he went back to his place in the triangle. Willow was being extra mean to me while her dad was there, but she'd told me to roll with the punches, follow her lead, and just play along. So I did. We sat in silence until the scar-faced man took a sharp inhale and paced the floor, leaving his triangle buds to stand there without a point.

"This is a simple task I need you to do." A grin reached across his face.

"Just follow my direction and you will be *fine*," he said.

"No!" I yelled. I figured that since she said that I was resistant, I should act resistant. He knitted his eyebrows. Willow lowered her head and managed a smirk.

"Willow, stop this!" She got up and grabbed my arm more softly than she should've and twisted it behind my back with as little force as possible, but I could tell trying to look rough and be soft at the same time wasn't that easy. The scar-faced man went back to his place at the tip of the triangle.

"Execution!" he yelled, and the rest of his triangle crew came marching for me in one line—each foot stomping to the same beat, every blink at the same time, and every move sharp and exact. They inched closer and closer until I closed my eyes with fear.

DNA? I Don't Think So!

The men picked me up and set me on a chair that looked like the one at my dental office. No sharp tools in sight, but there were other things like weapons around, which, in my opinion, were just as bad. I was strapped down to the chair and hoped that I would be able to wiggle out. I didn't know Willow's plan. All I knew was that I had to roll with the punches, follow her lead, and just play along. I squirmed, half-hoping to actually break from these straps. The triangle re-formed around my chair, and the scar-faced man stood over me holding Q-tips.

"Don't worry. We won't need these unless the first option doesn't work out. Willow," he said.

Willow grabbed a needle that I apparently missed and handed it to him.

"Open wide," he said.

I held my mouth shut, and I wasn't trying to roll with the punches. I was actually scared for my poor mouth. I think that Willow thought that I was doing a good job resisting him, because she grinned and nodded. He snapped his fingers, and one of his triangle men walked forward. He pried my mouth open and put in a mouth guard so big my cheeks were sore in ten seconds.

Willow stepped forward and watched the operation very closely. As he put the needle in my mouth and approached under my tongue, where I guess the best saliva was, I looked away for a second, seeing a figure in the corner dressed in all black. Before I could get a better look at the person, Willow grabbed his wrist and twisted it so hard I heard a cracking sound, and I wondered if his wrist broke. He groaned. His needle dropped from his hand onto the floor and shattered.

"No!" he yelled. Willow pushed through the crowd of shocked triangle men and unstrapped me. I got up and ran. She ran with me. We ran in the same route, but before we reached the front of the bakery, Willow stopped.

"Uhh, I can't," she said.

"Why not?" I asked, urging her on.

The triangle troop was catching up.

"That's my dad, Harper. Would you run from *your* dad? I mean, I already hurt him," she pointed out.

"Um, yes?" I tried to persuade her even though I was lying. "If he were an evil person trying to throw a needle in my friend's mouth!" I added.

"He'll catch me anyway," she said.

I guess I was advancing through the spy phases, 'cause I did something Savannah would have. I pulled Willow by the arm and studied a nearby fence.

I thought about throwing Willow up over the fence, but the top was a little pointy, and I really didn't trust this spark thing. So I did this thing I saw on TV once where one person puts their hands together and kneels down a bit, then the other person steps on their hands as a boost to get high or climb something. I put my hands together and waited for Willow to know what I was doing, but of course she didn't. I rolled my eyes as she looked at me like I was crazy.

"Look, just follow me!" I demanded more than asked, sounding somewhat like Kaleb.

We scaled the gate and got to the roof. I hid behind an air turbine and started to think. Normally I always think in silence, but this would have to do. Thinking led to phase three. I knew that this usually took hours, and I was going to be caught. So I trusted myself and waited for the triangle troop to come. Willow stood beside me, panting.

The triangle troop came sooner or later, and this time they were in full-on fighting gear. Willow and I walked out from behind the air turbine, and the triangle troop jumped out at us. I side-stepped, and Willow punched the lights out of a few, but just as fast, a few more came up the roof. We fought for a whole five minutes and I was already drenched in sweat. My head was burning from being in the sun, my goosebumps practically melted.

Why did the sun automatically come out? I figured out that my Converse weren't as good for fighting as I thought. My feet were burning as they rubbed against the bottom of my shoes. Then it happened. My vision got fuzzy, my temples were throbbing, and my palms were hot. A swoosh of color passed my eyes, then I was in a rainbow cyclone making me dizzy and feel like mush.

My limbs were not moving at all. I was still as stone. Finally everything stopped, and I could see myself doing backflips and using spy gadgets with no flaws. Then I fell through the floor with a loud crash and came back to life. I was standing pencil-straight with my eyes dry, like I hadn't blinked the whole time. Willow looked shocked and amazed at the same time.

"How did you do that?" she asked.

I looked around and saw that while I was doing whatever I was doing, I had beaten up the triangle troop. A dirty hand slapped onto the roof, and the body of the scar-faced man was pushed up. He sighed and wheezed. He cleared his throat and straightened his suit, which didn't do much; it was wrinkled and smeared with dirt. I readied my fists and waited for him to strike. But he just stood there.

"I am sorry, Willow. And Harper. But I need your DNA. So just let me have it." He wasn't really sorry, I could tell. He inched closer, and I moved backward. Willow stood as still as ice.

"Dad, why?" she sniffled. "Dad, why are you doing this?" she asked.

He blinked, and we sat there in silence. "W-well I, I...I have to do this! You just don't understand. It's for the better. If I have power, then no spy will ever get hurt again."

"You can't guarantee that," she snapped.

"What?" he asked.

"You CANNOT guarantee that no other spy can get hurt if you have power over all of them!" she yelled.

"Says who?" he asked.

"I say so. What do you think you'll gain if you take power over all of these people?" she asked.

Men, women, kids, teenagers, even senior citizens were watching us—two thirteen-year-old kids and a middle-aged man—talk about this crazy spy agency. A boy with shaggy black hair, a green T-shirt, and ripped zipper jeans was recording us. Willow and her dad didn't notice. I tried to tell Willow, but she wasn't listening.

A news van pulled up, and the news reporter jumped out of the van as quick as a blink. Reading her expression, I could tell she hadn't had a good news story to report in a while. She flicked back her flatironed hair, straightened her cream blouse, and carefully brushed her penciled-in eyebrows.

"This is LAE News, and I am Gabriella Jordans. I am reporting a...a, uh, roof scene including two young girls and a man on a roof," I heard her say. She turned toward the teenage boy and asked him, "What do you think this scene will do to this beloved city and this bakery?"

The boy talked low and deep so I couldn't hear him. But I think the news lady was impressed. She nodded and smiled until his mouth stopped moving.

"Crazy how one town can change so much after an incident like this happens. Now to you, Devin."

I looked around and saw a man standing behind the building talking to a camera.

"...we have firefighters and police coming to the scene," he said. I glanced at Willow, and they were still talking, I *had* to break this up.

"Okay, you two, the authorities are coming. So I don't think we want to end up in that situation." They understood right away, but we couldn't do anything.

I made the bold choice and told them, "Jump."

I stood at the edge of the roof, looked down, and got a little dizzy. People in the crowd were screaming a bunch of things at us.

One lady said, "Please, child, wait for the firefighters to help you down! You have a lot to live for! In fact, back in my day..." She went on and on.

Willow was running across the roof and jumped down. Her messy bun went free, and her hair went flying. The scar-faced man was sitting at the edge, trying to climb down, but with his dress shoes and hurt wrist, he couldn't get a good grip.

"Scar-faced man, you have to jump!" I told him.

He looked up at me. "Excuse me?" He was obviously offended.

"Uh," I started.

"The name is Benjamin."

I looked him up and down. He looked like a Cedric. But I didn't have time to obsess over his name. I grabbed his arm and pulled him up.

"Owwww! What is wrong with you?" I realized I was pulling his injured arm.

"Uh, sorry." I pulled him up, and together we ran and jumped off the roof, meeting Willow, who was sitting on the floor panting.

The news man, Devin, saw us and covered the mic to say, "Oooh, I am going to get promoted before Gabriella this time!" Then he uncovered the mic and started walking toward us. We got up and ran.

I could've sworn I heard his khakis rip as he chased us. We reached a dead end in an alley.

"Oh, no. I'm on camera," muttered Benjamin. He took off his dress shoes and threw them at the camera. Since Willow hurt his wrist, he had to use his left arm, and his aim was TERRIBLE! He missed the camera and hit a wall. He missed the camera*man* and hit the news reporter.

We were cornered, and I could hear the police and firefighters' cars approaching. I focused on family and pain, then the rush of colors came. Images of Simon came to me, and the memories of him being a brat came to me. Memories of the void council, Principal Kaleb, and, for some reason, my dentist came to me. This was a spark. I'd made my own spark happen!

Then it stopped. Right when I mentioned my accomplishment to myself, it stopped. I felt a little stronger. Then I remembered: *Simon is a brat.* All I had to do to bring memories of him back was be a brat. I didn't know how, though. I looked around me to find something useful. Willow saw me looking around, so she reached in her jacket and threw the dog whistle to me. Lousy shot. It landed in a muck puddle next to me. I gagged at it and slowly picked it up. I blew, but muck and mud came out. I almost threw up. Then I blew it again.

My lips quivering, I threw it back on the ground and silently swore that I would never, ever put my mouth on a dog whistle I'd found on the street again. The news man looked side to side, and nothing happened.

"Again, I am Devin Cambel and this is the breaking news of two troubled tweens and a mentally ill—"He was cut off.

"Rrrrugh! Ruff! Rrrrugh!" A dog came running down the alleyway as if waiting for a call—wait. No, not any dog. UMMA came running down the alleyway barking her head off. Then Devin went talking to the camera.

"Oh my God, and an evil dog!" he said with a girly scream.

"...mentally ill madman and two tweens; what will this city do? This is Channel 7 live!" he said professionally.

"Okay, and cut. You edit that out," he said.

He walked away, not even helping us. I don't know where he thought he was going because Umma chased close behind him, and he went running down the street with ripped pants and a crazed dog chasing him, and he was still holding his mic. Willow took my hand and Benjamin's hand, and we all ran. We ran fast, then slow, then fast, then slow.

When we reached the car, the people were gone. They were all out looking for us. I hopped in the backseat and sighed, not of relief, but of exhaustion. Making my own spark happen was tiring. Willow hopped in the front seat, and Benjamin sat next to her. We drove. I don't know where we were headed, but we drove and drove and drove until it got dark. I started to wonder where Umma was.

A Black Mask

We drove for miles until we reached the spy agency. It looked lifeless and boring. The outdoor lights that lit up the gate I'd once tried to break through-were out, and the place looked like a ghost house.

"Why are you being so nice?" I asked Benjamin. He looked at me and turned back.

"I am just softening up until I can...find a different way to carry out my plan." (In other words, "My daughter spoke to me, and I am thinking about changing my mind, so I am being nice because my daughter is making me feel guilty.") I shrugged like that response was okay (which it wasn't), and I waited for us to arrive at the campus.

SCREECH! BOOM! CLAP! WHAM! And our car lost all four wheels. We were turned sideways, and the only thing keeping me alive was my seatbelt. Glass shattered all over the car, and Willow was perfectly still. She wasn't moving or talking. Her dad was turned all the way around in his chair and hugging it like it was the end of his life. Come to think of it, I felt that way, too. A shadow walked in circles around our car, putting its hands along the rims of the wheels that lay around the car. I could see everything around me, yet I wasn't moving too much. The person wore a black cloth that hung all the way down to their ankles. I held my breath.

The person kept circling. Soon, I was sure my face was tomato red and my veins were popping out of my head. I exhaled so deeply the person flinched and pulled out a gadget. It was faint purple and shaped like a gun.

The person shot it at the car, and our car was being yanked across the yard. Rolling, tumbling, bouncing, twirling—so much I felt sick. The car came to a stop after seconds of pulling. I saw the gate out of our shattered window. Whoever this was was really going to get it.

My head was throbbing, and my stomach was bubbling. The hand came through the car window and got a hold of Willow's leg, which was hanging over the steering wheel. Willow was picked up, and I heard the person grunt as they set her down. The person found Benjamin's arm and pulled it up to the point where the light from the moon showed his face. They immediately dropped his arm. Then they grabbed my collar and yanked me up.

This person wore a black cloth mask over their mouth, but they started crying under the mask. I was super confused and scared. My hands were trembling, and my eyes filled with tears. The person ripped off their mouth cover, and I saw my mom! Her skin was smudged with dirt as if she'd been digging like a gopher.

"M-m-m-" I couldn't even say the name. I was sobbing, and my mom yanked me up into her arms. I just melted. I started to vent. "I missed you, Mom." She didn't even correct me by saying Mami.

"Shhh, *mi hija*." My mom kept hugging me.

"I—I have so many questions," I choked. All of my questions rushed through my head. *Where's Dad, Simon, and Umma? How are you working as a vet and a boss of a company? Where have you been hiding? Do you know Savannah? How is Savannah?* But I couldn't ask a word of them. We just kept hugging and crying.

Sadly, the moment was ruined by Benjamin, who loudly interrupted us.

"Ahem? *Ow!*" Willow pinched her dad. I wanted to go back to hugging. But my mom stopped, wiped her eyes, and looked Benjamin up and down.

"Benji," she said, narrowing her eyes.

Willow and I stepped back to see what was happening.

"How do they know each other?" Willow asked me. She had less damage than I thought she would—only a scratch on her hand.

"I was about to ask you the same thing," I said.

"Well, maybe since your mom owns this spy company, my dad doesn't like her. Or because my dad kidnapped your mom," she shrugged.

"I didn't even know my mom owned a spy company!" I answered.

"Oh, mija, I've owned this place for a long time," Mom said sweetly.

"But don't you work at the veterinarian office?" I asked. But instead of answering me, she turned all of her focus back to Benjamin.

They looked at each other competitively.

Savannah?

They just kept staring at each other that way.

"Hey? We *are* still here." Willow waved her hand in front of her dad's face.

"Oh,uh. I apologize for our past, but I am a *new man!*" Benjamin put his hands up as if that were proof.

"Of course you are. Just like you were in New Zealand. And Spain? Do I need to mentio—" She got cut off.

"Not that way, Elena. I am an *actual* new man. Ask my daughter!" he gestured to Willow.

"Your baby, Willow? My, have you grown!" Mom walked around Willow in a circle.

"*Quit* the small talk! How do you know each other?" Willow got down to the point.

"Missions," they both said in unison.

My mom continued. *"Join Spy Society Number Eight! It's great,"* she said in a commercialized tone.

"Who puts out ads for a spy agency?" Willow asked.

"I d—" Benjamin started.

"It was a rhetorical question." She put her hand up.

As they went on, Willow and I snuck away to my dorm room.

"Savannah," I started, "we're home!" I looked around the room. Savannah wasn't in sight.

"Hello?" Willow called out.

"I think she is playing a prank on us," I told Willow.

"Yeah, pranks *always* end up fine, don't

they?" She pointed to the spot on her head where Savannah had smacked her, though it was no longer pink.

"Technically, that wasn't a prank. She was delusional," I shrugged.

Willow sat up and held up Savannah's hair pin.

"Okay?" I said.

Willow looked out the window.

"Our parents are about to vaporize each other." She squinted.

"Oh, my!" I said, looking out of the window.

"I'm gonna go and protect both of them!" She ran out of the room, and I kept looking under the bed. *BUMP!* I hit something. I pulled it out. A safe! The code had to be four characters long. I looked around. Nothing. I looked under the safe, and there was nothing. I shifted the box, and when the moonlight shone directly on the bottom, the password, written in invisible ink, showed up. 2-6-9-4. I put it in and opened it. There was an amulet and a diary. The diary was titled, "Savannah Tucker's Diary. Do NOT Touch!"

I pulled out the diary wondering, and hesitated, but I opened it.

Eye Spy 2

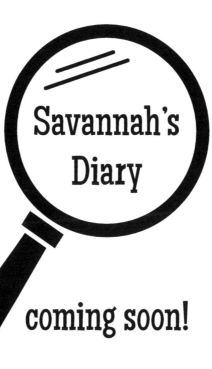

Savannah's
Diary

coming soon!

Acknowledgements

Dear Readers,
Writing this book was an extreme accomplishment, and I will value this day forever. I want to give a special thank you to my mom, Delilah Clayborne, the woman who helped me so much throughout the process of making *"Eye Spy"*. I am really grateful for my co-author, Kallie Harris! She was a HUGE part of drawing the images and helping with the story. Kallie is more than a help, but an inspiration to me. I am so thankful for her, and I value our friendship. I also want to show my love for Lyndi

Clayborne, my loving, supportive sister, who was always looking over my shoulder when I wrote with Kallie. I want to thank my dad, Leon Clayborne, for also supporting me and helping me, from editing, to finding the right questions for an interview. I couldn't be more ecstatic with this accomplishment.

Co-author

LaiC.

Writing this book was a life-changing experience. I made a friend and an amazing accomplishment. It's amazing how a pen pal can turn into a co-author, then into a best friend. The first person I want to thank is my mom, Carol Harris, for giving me and Lailah the idea to become pen pals in the first place. Next, I want to thank Lailah Clayborne, my co-author. Thank you so much for being a friend! I also would like to thank my dad,

Terence Harris, for inspiring me to sketch and teaching me all he knew about it. Of course the internet gets its credit as well! For letting me and my co-author connect from a long distance. To all the *You're muted* and *You glitched out* moments!

Co-author
Illustrator

A little thank you from both of the young authors

Together, we'd like to thank Akilah Trinay, our publishing consultant! She played a big role in helping us accomplish our dream.

About the Authors

LAILAH CLAYBORNE

From the bubbly age of eight, Lailah Clayborne knew she was born to write. Two years later, amid the pandemic, her parents arranged for her to become a pen pal, [inserting Kallie into her life]. The two have been writing together ever since. Lailah has a big heart and an even greater imagination. She is a young leader, sharing her gifts with all she can, from assisting her dad with beach cleanups to giving out food and care packages with her grandmother at church. She hopes her writing will inspire other young people to try their hobby and make it professional. Lailah's greatest accomplishment is being a big sister to her two siblings.

KALLIE HARRIS

Kallie Harris is a student, artist, and now author. Becoming pen pals with Lailah changed her life in the best way. Her parents encouraged her to use her artistic talent to write and illustrate her first book. When she is not writing, some of her hobbies include: cooking, reading, crafting, and drawing. "Something I want people to know about me is that I am a ten-year-old girl who pursued one of the things on her bucket list: publishing a book."

Eye Spy: Harper's Beginning is the first installment of this series from this co-writing duo.

For more information and updates follow @unitedpenpals on Instagram or email unitedpenpals@gmail.com.

Made in the USA
Monee, IL
10 October 2021

798bc92e-8d2f-4956-b1fa-c7ec51460915R01